To Nancy,

Sometimes we don't
know it all!

EVERYTHING
I KNOW

Cliff Fazzolari

Clifford James Fazzolari

DEDICATION:

This book is dedicated to my family. I've been blessed since day one, and together we have all built a life of trust and understanding. When you speak of family it should be all about the love. For me it is, and I thank you, Kathy, Matt, Jake & Sam.

TABLE OF CONTENTS

PART 1

CHAPTER 1 – DECEMBER 3, 2014

Good decisions come from experience and experience comes from bad decisions.
Anonymous

Time may eventually build a bridge to take you clear of a great tragedy, but more often than not, the bridge has been erected on a flimsy base, and the slightest movement may obliterate the foundation.

Jenna's three-word message, left on an answering machine that spoiled a lovemaking session with my current girlfriend, was simple.

I need you.

I was hoping that Valerie had not heard the words, but with my tongue poised in mid-air, in the spot just below her navel, she struggled to break free.

"That was Jenna, wasn't it?" she asked.

"Yeah, I think so," I said. "I don't care."

Valerie was up and out of the bed.

I was able to see the curve of her back clearly because she made a grand gesture of turning that back to me. She grabbed the yellow sheet off the bed and covered her lower half as she sighed heavily, and headed for the bathroom. I flopped back onto the bed, no longer hearing Valerie's words of complaint. The only three words stuck in my head were spinning in a dizzy loop as though the needle were stuck in the groove of a record.

I need you!

Valerie disappeared into the bathroom.

From behind the closed door I heard her rummaging through the medicine cabinet for the toothbrush that she'd left behind. She didn't live with me full-time, but that was also a major part of the argument that was about to happen.

Despite the fact that she never met Jenna, Valerie hated her with all the passion she could muster. That was easy enough, considering that Jenna, my ex-wife, the woman who bore my child, a child that lived only seven weeks, was a famous soap opera and B-movie actress, and according to People Magazine one of the hundred most beautiful people in the world. There was little I could say through that closed door that wouldn't sound desperate.

"Come on back to bed," I tried. "Let's talk about it."

Of course, Valerie didn't answer right away. If I could guess, what she did do was knock my little blue cup off the sink and onto the floor. I listened to it clatter across the tiles as Valerie cursed loud enough for me to understand that she was royally pissed.

"What am I guilty of here?" I asked. "Having a telephone? She called me. I haven't even called her back!"

I had thought of getting rid of the damn home line. This about clinched it.

"But you will!" Valerie screamed. "You will run right to the phone after I leave and then I'll lose you to her again. In fact, I never really had you! What's it been? Seven years? But she calls and good old Sal will come running!"

I covered my head with the pillow. Ten minutes previous I had been mere moments away from making love to a woman who now wanted to rip my throat out. Lord knows that she had her reasons.

It had been ten years since I met Jenna in the parking lot of a 7/11 convenience store. Jenna had backed a white Mustang convertible into a parking spot at the precise moment that I had pulled straight in with my beat-up yellow Ford pickup truck. Our eyes locked, and despite the fact that I wasn't much of a believer in love at first sight, I was as they say, head over heels. Jenna's blue eyes sparkled as she smiled at me, and my first thought was that she had laughing eyes. Jenna had the most incredible, sky-blue, laughing eyes.

"Come here often?" she asked.

"It *is* convenient," I said. "And I'm sure glad I stopped."

From the moment that I met her I knew that Jenna was probably more trouble than she was worth, but I also knew that she was most likely headed for superstardom. There wasn't a man in the world that could look away from her. When I met her she had shoulder-length hair, the face of an angel, and that devilish, intoxicating smile.

"You wanna' get a drink?" she asked playfully.

I often wonder how my life would have turned out had I refused her offer for that drink.

The bathroom door swung open and Valerie stood before me. She was dressed in a cranberry red blouse with tan pants. The wish that she'd come back to bed was instantly dashed.

"Do you remember what Jenna said to you when your baby died?" Valerie asked. "Do you remember how she treated you?"

I hadn't expected Valerie to empty both barrels so quickly, but the fact that she did infuriated me.

"Of course, I remember. I can't believe you think just because she needs me, I'm going to run back with arms wide open. Give me a little credit here, huh?"

I threw the covers off and felt around on the floor for my underwear. If we were going to argue I wasn't going to do it naked.

But there wasn't going to be an argument.

Valerie ran from the bedroom, down the hall of my small ranch house and out the front door before I even had the chance to pull on a pair of shorts.

That first night in Jenna's company had ended with a kiss on the cheek and the promise of another date. We had sipped white wine on a bar on the shores of the Atlantic as the sun sank in the sky just over my right shoulder.

"You get one wish for a job, what is it?" Jenna asked.

"I want to write a column that'll appear in every newspaper in the country," I said. "I want to call it *Everything I Know*."

"That's brilliant!" Jenna said. "So, do it."

She traced the rim of her glass with the index finger of her right hand. Her long, elegant finger with the bright red nail polish worked the glass as though Jenna actually *loved* the glass.

"You get one wish for a woman. What would she look like?"

I was being set up by the question, but I was smart enough to formulate the right answer. I closed my eyes as though I were imagining the perfect woman.

"My perfect woman would have shoulder-length honey blond hair, and bright blue eyes that look like weather. She would have a small waist, stand about five-seven, aspire to be a movie star, and that's about it."

"Really now," Jenna said.

"And big breasts," I added. "You can't forget the big boobs."

Jenna laughed uproariously. She had a laugh that sounded like music.

"She sounds an awful lot like me," she whispered, as her finger returned to the rim of the glass.

"She certainly does," I said. I leaned in for the kiss, and Jenna met my lips with her left cheek.

"Patience, my dear, patience," she said.

"That was so long ago," I said to the now empty room. "A lifetime ago."

I pulled a pair of jeans on, and headed to the fenced in back yard. My dog, Max, jumped for my attention and I took all eighty pounds of the golden lab to my chest as he tried to lick my face. Valerie was 'allergic' to dogs and treated Max with absolute disdain.

"She's gone," I said, and as I said it I wondered if it were a permanent thing, or if I truly cared. Twenty minutes ago I had cared, but the three-word message certainly changed that.

Max headed to the door and the comfort of the heated house. Despite the fact that it was unseasonably warm, it was still a

Baltimore night in December. Unseasonably warm was still just the low 40's.

I looked to the evening sky. The moon was riding high and the clouds offered just enough of a break to see a few glittering stars.

Why did Jenna need me?

There was only one way to find out.

***

I couldn't help but stare at the telephone. The black cordless was right beside me, begging me to pick it up and dial the number. Although I hadn't spoken to Jenna in years, she would always forward her latest cell phone number to me in a text or e-mail. I memorized the number each time, but never had the guts to call.

Our marriage was a lifetime ago and it didn't really work because of the pain. Yet I knew the contours of her beautiful body like the roads upon a map. The very essence of her was in my veins and pulsed through my body with each heartbeat. I assumed that she felt the exact same way. I chased the heat of her blood. We spent long, passionate nights together and we playfully shared our days. Our life seemed perfect in every way until the moment when she announced that she was pregnant.

On that very Monday morning I was called into the editor's office at the *Baltimore Sun*. John Paige, a behemoth of a man who never met a sausage sandwich he could resist cleared a mound of newspapers off of a chair so that I could sit at the desk across from him.

"You're getting your chance," Paige said. He had a sloppy goatee beard that looked a tad uncomfortable to me. As he said the words all I could think of was buying him a razor for Christmas.

"We are going to run your weekly column idea for the next three months. *Everything I Know* huh? That's a little narcissistic don't you think?"

"I suppose," I said. "I'm doing it with the greater good in mind," I said.

Paige laughed in my face.

"Dream big, right Piseco? I can see it now: you'll be on Oprah Winfrey like that fat Doctor Phil, spewing your bullshit to the masses. Your name will be up in lights: Sal Piseco, 'The Greatest Thinker of All-Time.'"

I couldn't get over the fact that the 330-pound man sitting across from me was comfortable calling Dr. Phil fat.

"I appreciate the opportunity," I said. "Is there anything else I can do for you?"

"Yeah, what's the first gem about? I have to let the dumb-ass bosses who believe in you know what you're writing about."

It was my turn to laugh. Paige was playing with his food-stained red necktie.

"Belief," I said. "I'm going to be writing about belief in oneself."

Paige stuck his finger in the mouth as though he were trying to gag himself. "Oh puke," he said. "Good luck, dreamer."

I was absolutely bursting with excitement as I made my way back to my office. Writing the column was something that I'd pitched to the big bosses for years. I wasn't about to let anyone down, least of all myself. Holding onto belief would be the perfect first column.

I spent the rest of the afternoon scratching an outline and trying to get a hold of Jenna. My telephone calls went unanswered, however. It was the days before texting and social media so I was at the mercy of her return call. It just wasn't coming, and it was driving me up the wall.

I battled the drive time traffic concentrating on how I could piece the column together. My words of wisdom could make a difference in the lives of my readers.

At that time Jenna and I weren't officially living together, but she was at my apartment more often than not. She had moved her clothes in, taking up most of the space in what used to be my closet so I figured that the rest of her wouldn't be too far behind.

In the early evening, I pulled my car into the driveway in front of the townhouse that I was renting. Jenna's white Mustang was parked in my spot, and my heart did a slight leap in my chest. I couldn't wait to tell her about my big break. What I hadn't expected was to see Jenna sitting outside, at the picnic table. She was wearing my light brown Carhartt jacket, and she was smoking a cigarette. She didn't look up as I parked my pick-up, slid the keys into my front pocket and whistled as I walked towards her. Jenna's head was bowed, and as I got closer, I heard her sobbing. The glory of finally getting my own column was swept away on the light breeze as a sense of panic gripped my heart and mind.

"Jenna? Honey, what's wrong?"

She jumped as though I'd hit her with a stun gun.

"Jesus, you scared the shit out of me!"

Her eyes were bright red and a violent sniffle preceded another puff on the cigarette that was burning dangerously close to the filter.

"You don't even smoke," I said.

I wasn't sure that was the most important thing to say but I had to start somewhere.

Jenna didn't answer right away. She reached down and scratched her left leg, just below the tattoo of the rose above her ankle.

"I'm fucking pregnant," she cried. "I've never smoked in my life, but now I don't want to give it up for nine months."

I dropped to one knee in front of her. I reached for her hands, but she tossed the cigarette aside and buried her painted fingers in the pockets of the oversized jacket.

"This is awful," she whispered. "I'm *supposed* to be an actress."

I took my time in formulating an answer, knowing that whatever came out of my mouth next would be long remembered. I had to give a perfect, honest answer, but truthfully, what was honest? I wasn't even sure if I were happy or sad. Was this the greatest news in the world, or something that would ruin the love we shared?

The wind gusted and sent a quick shiver down my spine. Jenna seemed to bury herself deeper in the jacket. I felt the wet grass seeping through the knees of my dress pants, but I slowly placed my right hand under Jenna's chin to lift her beautiful face. Looking into her eyes, I said the first thing that came to mind, and it was a perfectly honest response to the situation.

"I love you more than I've ever loved anyone," I whispered. A whiff of her sweet perfume helped me realize that I had said the exact right thing.

Jenna emitted a sound that was half-laugh, half-sob but even with the red eyes and red nose she was every bit as beautiful to me as the first time I'd seen her in the parking lot of the convenience store.

"Pregnant!" She yelled. "I hate kids!"

We both laughed and it suddenly occurred to me that I was on my knees in perfect marriage proposal position. Still I needed to give her time to arrive at her own conclusion.

"I've known it for a few days," she said. "For the first time in my life I was late. This is just horrible."

She didn't want me to solve the riddle for her. I just stayed there poised in front of her with my wet knees on my mind. Jenna rocked forward and her teeth chattered, and she sobbed her next line.

"Don't you dare ask me to marry you," she cried. "I just won't do it."

**

The very next day my first *Everything I Know* column was printed in the <u>Baltimore Sun</u>. the column took over the lead league in letters to the editor, as my words seemed to strike a chord with the general public. John Paige took the news hard. My column would be a weekly event.

Everything I Know About Belief

One of the more disconcerting things in the world is to meet someone who has lost faith or belief. You have to have faith in faith and you have to believe in belief. It's often times easier said than done, though, because there are ill winds all around that corrode the soul and block the channels from which love and creativity flow. I know. I've spent some time in the abyss. Yet through painful bouts of reasoning, and more than a few moments trying to get every last drop out of a bottle of chilled Grey Goose, I've kind of come to understand a few things lately:

1. *You should never really settle for something less than who you want to be. It's easy to slip off the tracks and stay nestled in the weeds, instead of getting back on track. No one ever aspires to "live in a van down by the river," as Chris Farley, once so eloquently put it in a <u>Saturday Night Live</u> sketch, but people end up there, and they stay there, because they lose faith in themselves.*

2. *You should rejoice in the achievements of others. This is a tricky one because a lot of times we look at others and think, 'How'd that dumb %&*#$@ become so lucky?' Channel the positive results achieved by others and put them to work for yourself. My father told me early on in life to compete only with myself. Great advice. Playing that game within your own mind will help you blow off all self-imposed limits.*

3. *Do you still believe that all things are possible? I know a lot of people who get stuck in the muck and mire of not being able to do something because they believe (there's that word again) that they cannot stay out of their own way. There are really good people out there, who suffer bad event after bad event, because they can't figure how to rise above. The reason why is because they accept their fate as the best the can do, or be.*

4. *So how to move that rubber tree plant? There are so many clichés and you hear Dr. Phil and Oprah spouting about all of them, but there are things that work. Like clearing your mind of negativity. Or finding faith in a power that is larger than the little life you're leading - faith in God Above allows some of this to make sense, right? And visualizing that success (in any endeavor) can be*

achieved. And finally, by then doing your best through good old-fashioned hard work. It's the only way.

You can buy the Mega Million ticket and dream that the numbers will change all that's wrong. Or you can believe in yourself, and make some of the lesser (more important) dreams come true.

That's Everything I Know about Belief.

I reread that first column as I stared at the telephone wondering if I should respond to Jenna's request for help. I *did* love Valerie now. I certainly owed her a moment of consideration. Plucking the phone up and calling Jenna would change everything. Valerie knew it. I knew it. Hell, even Max, panting beside me knew it. It was at that precise moment that the telephone rang, causing me to nearly jump clear of my rotting skin.

CHAPTER 2

Anything looked at closely becomes wonderful.
A.R. Ammons

I met the third ring of the telephone with a startled stare. What would I say to her by way of greeting? I thought of the child we made together. The beautiful, magical, defective child that died before he ever truly lived. My heart sank. I was ready to hear her voice.

"Are you going to take my mother to her appointment?" Valerie asked.

I held down the sigh of disappointment that worked its way up through my chest cavity. Valerie's tone wasn't only confrontational it was downright nasty.

"Of course I'll take her," I said. "I'm her radiation buddy."

For the better part of two weeks, I had picked Valerie's mother up and waited for her as she received treatments for breast cancer.

"That's good," Valerie said. Her voice had softened a bit, but there was a still question waiting out there for me to answer and we both knew it.

"Her appointment is for ten o'clock. Perhaps you can take her to lunch afterwards. She loves the melts at Denny's."

Valerie was beating around the bush and we both knew it. Of course, her mother wanted to go to Denny's. We had shared ten of the ham and Swiss cheese melts over the last two weeks.

"I didn't call her back," I said. "But I have to, you know. It won't change us, Val. I just have to."

"I know," Valerie said. She was nearly whispering now. The anger of this morning replaced by a resigned fear that was palpable through the telephone line. "Remember though, I love you more than anyone you've ever met."

She hung up the phone and her words, and the click of the phone, resonated in my mind.

I need you!
Damn it!

I dressed in a pair of jeans and a beige pullover shirt. The shirt was wrinkled, but it never mattered much. Dressing poorly was expected of me. My column was due by the end of the day, but it was sitting in the hard drive of my computer, ready to be sent with a single click of the mouse. I loved the days when the column was due because it was usually complete and I didn't have to go near the offices. The success of the column had allowed me plenty of perks. I was free to take my girlfriend's mother to the 'poison tank' and out to Denny's.

Max stood by the front door. He was more than ready to go with me. He lived life for the rides in the car, but he also seemed to understand that sometimes he just couldn't go along.

"Not today, buddy," I said. "I have too much to do."

I rubbed Max's ears and he playfully licked my right wrist.

"I'll be back soon," I said. "If Jenna calls tell her I got her message and I don't know what the hell to do. Try and stay off the couch."

I grabbed my keys and headed for the door. I snuck one more look at the phone before I headed out. From out of the corner of my eye, I saw Max make the leap onto the brown cushions of the couch.

"Dream well, buddy."

The elation of being a first-time father lasted for all of about two hours. Jenna suffered through the delivery as the biggest tears I had ever seen rolled down her face, and mixed with the sweat, the elation and my loving embrace. The doctor, a man named Nicolmeti asked me to snip the cord, but I refused. That was his job. I simply wanted to hold Jenna and bask in the fact that I had witnessed a true miracle. Of course, I cried as well. I was a father. I would be able to do all of the things that my father never truly felt compelled to do.

It's funny that one of the places where you learn new words that you don't want to know the meaning of is in the halls of a hospital. The slightly blue-colored toes, fingers and lips in baby Anthony came with a name.

"We may be dealing with cyanotic heart disease," Nicolmeti explained to me. The colorful walls of the pediatric unit were in direct contrast to the dark cloud that I imagined rising in my chest. I spied a painted image of a cartoon fish swimming to a pool of bigger fish. It looked like the baby fish was trying to join its family.

"Cyanotic heart disease is a congenital heart defect that affects about 8 in every 1,000 babies born. 85% of the time newborns with a congenital heart defect survive well into adulthood," Nicolmeti's lips were moving rapidly. He was a balding, middle-aged man with a small pair of round glasses that conjured up a professorial look of undeniable intelligence. He had delivered the most amazing news of my life to me, and now he was obliterating it with his follow-up message. Despite the rising storm, I tried to remain even-keeled.

"So what happens now?" I asked.

"We fix it," Nicolmeti said. "We are going to take Anthony for an echocardiogram or an electrocardiogram. That will be up to the cardiologist."

Nicolmeti wiped a bead of sweat from his forehead. He was speaking in whispered tones, and studying my face to see if I registered even a snippet of what he was telling me. I wasn't. All I could think of was Jenna and how, if things didn't turn out perfectly, she would be crushed beyond all repair. The idea of a glowing mother had been a myth to me until I saw how beautifully Jenna took to being pregnant.

"There are a number of treatment options available to us through the process. We have to take it a step at a time. The diagnosis was made rapidly and we are prepared to move forward."

Nicolmeti's hand went to my right shoulder. "You don't look so good yourself," he said. "Let's get you a seat and a glass of cold water."

Those last few words reached me in a dizzying spin of life that left me flat on the floor in the middle of that colorful hallway.

***

Valerie's mother, Elaine, was standing at the end of her driveway in White Marsh. The remembrances of Anthony's short life hammered at my sensibilities, but the breath of life that was the crumpled up woman who faced radiation treatment for breast cancer was about to blow through my life. I hit the unlock button to open the passenger side door, and Elaine lifted the door handle and got in. I knew better than to get out of the car. Elaine had told me a number of times that she didn't want to be treated as an invalid.

"Good morning," she said as she plopped into the passenger seat, undid a red scarf that had been keeping her neck warm, and smiled.

"Let's go blast my tits some more."

I had taken to calling Elaine 'Mom' and it was a fact that thrilled her to no end. I leaned to kiss her wrinkled left cheek.

"Good morning, Mom, there's nothing better than talking about your tits."

Elaine laughed, but the laugh was forced. Valerie told her about Jenna's phone call.

"How are you feeling?" I asked. I had driven her to her treatment on five days previous, but we had not spoken since.

"I'm all right," she said. "They keep blasting me with this shit though and eventually they're going to start me on fire. My right boob is one dose away from going up in flames."

Elaine was wearing a light blue, loose-fitting blouse over tan 'old lady' pants, as she called them. She opened her coat to show me all of this as I drove to the doctor's office at a strip mall in White Marsh.

"What's the column about this week?" she asked.

"Filling the empty spaces in your heart," I said. "It's everything I know about picking up the pieces."

"Why of course it is," Elaine said. "You're always *so* inspirational."

Elaine joked around so much that I wasn't sure if her last remark was a statement of fact or a backhanded sarcastic slap.

"When I write my memoir it's going to be called, 'I Know What I Know.'"

"That has best-seller written all over it," I said.

We both laughed, but given Elaine's love of life and the regret that had been hammered home through the years, I wasn't sure that she couldn't rise to the top of the NY Times list.

At 74 years old, Elaine had lived through it all. She'd married two men who treated her with utter disdain. The first man, Robert, who she hardly ever mentioned, had a gambling addiction and a taste for other women. His life had ended in a fiery, drunken one-car crash that brought three fire companies to the scene.

"I hope he suffered," was all Elaine would ever say.

The second man, Edward, who was Valerie and David's father, was a tad more responsible, but just a tad. Twelve years into the marriage, he decided that enough was enough, and he headed out of town leaving a simple note that said, 'I can't live like this anymore.'

"Good riddance to a real piece of shit," Elaine always mentioned. Edward suffered a massive heart attack and dropped like a bag of dirt on a city street, somewhere in California.

"You get what you get," was how Elaine explained it.

We continued the drive in a harried discussion of Obama and the healthcare bill that was threatening to cut the legs out of her radiation treatments.

"What kills me about those damn congressmen is that they all have the best fucking healthcare imaginable. Someone like me has to get her breasts blasted in a goddamn shopping mall."

I pulled the truck into our usual spot at the doctor's office. Elaine was exaggerating her poor healthcare, but not by much. The medical offices of O'Brien and Gerreti were nestled between Mina's Cleaning Service and Brady's Fence Company.

"Are we going to Denny's when I'm done?" Elaine asked.

"Of course," I said.

I made for the side door, fully intending at helping Elaine out of her side of the car, but she stopped me from moving by gently placing her left hand on my right arm.

"We got a minute," she said. "Talk to me about Jenna."

I slumped back in the seat and closed my eyes. I wasn't sure that I wanted to get into a discussion of a telephone call that I had not even returned yet.

"Come on," Elaine said. "Remember when my son moved to Germany and what a wreck I was? Remember how I listened to your life-affirming bullshit?"

I laughed heartily and opened my eyes to her smiling, wrinkled, beautiful face.

Elaine looked out the passenger-side window and pointed across the nearly empty parking lot to a brand new graffiti painting that advertised, 'Sex, Money & Murder.'

"Them sonuvabitches that paint that shit have some real talent," she said. "Instead of painting the city why don't they get jobs as graphic artists?"

"I don't know," I said. She had a legitimate point. The word 'Sex' was painted black, 'Money' was green of course, and 'Murder' was bright red and lettered larger than the rest.

"Hooligans," Elaine muttered under her breath. "Anyhow, Sal, the way I figure this, you have to play your cards right here. Valerie is understandably upset because she figures that you're going to run straight back to Jenna as her scent comes to your nose. I have my doubts that you'll behave in such a selfish manner, but I've been wrong before."

I started to protest, feeling that I needed to let Elaine know that I hadn't even returned the call, but Elaine was too quick for me. Her raised hand stifled my words.

"I know what I know. The other night I had a dream about my first husband. We were so young."

Elaine coughed and then took well over a minute to retrieve a handkerchief that she used to wipe her mouth.

"Anyway…this sucks by the way. I dreamed that Robert and I were still in love. In my dream we were lying in bed, laughing like a couple of kids. It could have happened, I suppose, because the dream seemed so real."

Elaine coughed again.

"I'm getting to the point," she said.

I laughed again, but I had to admit to myself that I was sort of on pins and needles. If Elaine had life advice, I wanted to hear it.

"I gave Robert everything he needed and still he flew the coup."

Elaine waited for my reaction. I had no intentions to 'fly the coup' as she so eloquently put it, but there was that chance, right?

"Remember, when you make that call, and you have to make the call by the way, that sometimes all you ever need is never quite enough. Jenna is going to offer you a chance at another sort of adrenalin rush. Do what you gotta' do, but don't leave tattered shit in your wake."

Elaine's hand on the door handle signaled an end to our little discussion.

"I can't wait to read your column today," she said. "Now let's go fry these tits like a couple of over-easy eggs. You'll call Jenna from the waiting room. Then we'll have something to talk about over lunch."

Elaine checked in at the front desk as I found my usual seat in the waiting area. I loved the seat closest to the door, away from the roar of the television and the two chatty receptionists, who talked incessantly of their boyfriends and which bars they would frequent after work. I had learned to avoid them and their bright pink uniforms and fake smiles. As I did every Tuesday, I raised a copy of my new column on my black, Droid cell phone, and read it for last minute changes.

Everything I Know About Peace

There has never been a person who has walked this planet who has came away unscathed. Just standing next to the person at the checkout line in the grocery store, and just listening, will allow you the opportunity to hear about some of the pain that living brings.

Just yesterday, a coworker spoke to me about a friend of his who was busy holding a memorial golf tournament for his son. The man's son had died of a traumatic brain injury when he fell down the stairs at college. My heart broke with the news of such an unspeakable tragedy that has left holes all over the county.

Just try reading the newspaper on a regular basis. Scan the obits and glance at the ages of the people who have died. For every man or woman listed there were hundreds of others affected by their lives. In some cases, there are thousands that will feel the void. Everyone that I have ever met is walking around with a hole in his or her heart. The heartbreak of life is unavoidable. Pain will be on the menu until this huge ball stops spinning.

What do we do with the voids? How do we fill the empty spaces? Believe it or not, there are choices to be made. We can eat ourselves into a coma, or do the same with drink. We can fill the hole in our heart with anger, eternal sadness, or hatred. We can drink, gamble, carouse, engage in all sorts of sexual deviant behavior, shoot people down (literally or figuratively), gossip, threaten and cajole.

There are so many freedoms afforded to us in this country, in this life, and in our own minds, that we can fill the voids anyway that we see fit. Religious services do a brisk business as they prey on people who are simply searching for an answer. That is why there are hundreds of robberies, break-ins, and murders every night. That is why people fill their evenings watching dogs fight or cocks fight, or why they drunk drive their butts home, not caring who or what they destroy along the way.

There are millions of people walking around like zombies. There is too much anger, hatred and jealousy, and there are so few viable avenues to chase the demons away. We all carry the seeds of self-destruction in our pockets and we spill those seeds, trying just to fill the empty space that is there just because we have lived.

I wish that I could say that I always fill the voids in my heart with love. I try to. I really do. At the very least, I have learned to recognize that the empty spaces need to be filled with things that allow me to feel better, not worse.

Through the years of my life, I have surrounded myself with people that I love, and people who love me. The idea is to suffer together, as a *team, until the other side come calling.*

Yet that is an easy thing to forget. It is simple to sink into an abyss as you attempt to burn out the traces of pain. Through my life, I have shed my skin so many times in an effort to become the man I need to be, and to make it sync up with the goodness of my heart.

I will continue to try because for some reason, today, I understand that the empty spaces must be filled. Sometimes the choices we make to fill the empty spaces present us with a new set of circumstances to self-destruct. Day after day. Moment after moment. No one promised that it would be easy.

That's 'Everything I Know' about finding some peace.

Satisfied that the column was ready, I closed the phone and tossed it from hand to hand for a minute. Elaine's treatment was just getting started. Was this where I wanted to make the call to Jenna? Could I even speak to her in the empty waiting room? I decided to jump in feet first. Elaine was right. It *had* to be done. I punched in the numbers as an overwhelming fear grew inside of me. Once the door was open, it could not be closed. Was I ready to change every aspect of my life?

This is Jenna! Thanks for calling! I've been thinking about you! Leave a message and I'll get back to you as soon as I can. Have a great day!

Her answering machine message was pure Jenna, as the caller glimpsed the sunshine that she brought with her to every conversation. It was a far cry from her *I need you* message of last night.

"Jenna, its Sal. If you need me, I'm here. Of course, I'm here. You're scaring me too, darling, and call as soon as you can."

I closed the phone and it immediately occurred to me that I had made a mistake in calling her darling, but that was always they way it had been with us. I had actually spent all of those years calling her my 'pretty darling.'

"Damn it," I whispered.

The two noisy receptionists were going back and forth about last night's showing of *American Idol*. I seriously doubted that they were among my readers. I spent the rest of my waiting time wishing that Jenna would return the call, but it didn't come.

A little less than half an hour later, Elaine emerged from behind the glass doors leading from the radiation area. She wore a smile, but she looked quite a bit more haggard than when she had stepped through those doors.

"Seven treatments left," she said. "Seven more damn treatments."

I got to my feet, but knew better than to grab her arm and help her to the door. Instead, I swung the front door open so that we could make our escape.

"Ready for the ham and cheese melt?" I asked.

Before Elaine could step out into the cold afternoon air, a young woman stepped into my line of vision. The woman, with her dark hair up in a bun was showing signs of pure distress as she guided an older version of herself through the doors. The older woman was in a wheelchair, and her crying jag was in full swing.

"I don't know why I have to do this," the old woman was saying. "How much longer am I going to live anyway? And you're bringing me in here to get blasted as if I'm a friggen' experiment!"

I locked eyes with the young woman who seemed more embarrassed than upset.

"Please Mom, don't make a scene."

"Make a scene!" the old woman screamed. "I just want to die in peace. Why won't you let me die in peace?"

The young woman guided the chair by me, rolling her brown eyes as she brushed by, a look of nervous worry on her face. It was at that precise moment that Elaine stepped in front of the chair. She lowered her mouth to the old woman's ear. The young woman glanced to me and I shrugged my shoulders as Elaine whispered her message. Suddenly, both of the radiation patients burst into laughter.

"Perfect!" the woman in the chair called out. "Let's do this," she said to her daughter. Once more, I shrugged.

"What was that all about?" I asked Elaine as we escaped into the cold afternoon air.

"Just filling empty spaces," Elaine said. "I know what I know."

CHAPTER 3

As soon as you trust yourself you will know how to live.
Johann Wolfgang von Goethe

The success of my written column was growing far and wide stretching well beyond the Baltimore city limits. 'Everything I Know' was a syndicated column that allowed me tremendous liberties in and around the offices. I spent a large part of my day promoting the weekly column on radio stations all across the land, and newspapers as far away as Seattle, Washington carried my words of wisdom. It could have gone to my head, I suppose, but it truly didn't. I saw the column for what it was. Simply put, it was just my spin on the dizzying, confusing pain that comes with living from day-to-day. The writing was successful only because I was putting a name to the pain. I considered all of this as Elaine plopped into the space in the booth across from me at Denny's.

"Isn't life a bitch?" Elaine asked as she picked up the menu, adjusted her glasses and coughed. "That old lady at the poison tank has no idea what the hell she's in for. They're going to blast her titties to kingdom come and she decided to do it because I told her a joke about dying."

"What was the joke?" I asked.

"I can't tell you," Elaine said. "You aren't ready."

The waitress stepped into position at the front of the table. Her nametag read Randi and she was a pretty, young girl who would have looked a lot better with a smile. "Something to drink?" she asked. We ordered our sodas and Randi left quickly.

"What a sourpuss," Elaine said. "So, what do we talk about today? Jenna didn't answer, right?"

I nodded.

"Then we need a topic of conversation." Elaine peered at me over the top of her glasses. "Do you want to tell me about your son?" she asked.

"It doesn't much sound like my idea of fun," I said. "Have you ever tried the 'Moons over My Hammy'?"

"No," Elaine said. "That makes me think I'm eating a piece of ass. Now don't change the subject."

Randi returned with our drinks, placed them in front of us, and stood before us with her pad at the ready.

"We'll have the ham and cheese melts with fries, both of us," Elaine said. "And you might try to turn that frown around, young lady; you look as if someone just pulled your pretty hair."

Randi took the menus from my hand and spun on her heels, heading away from the table.

"Miserable broad," Elaine said. "Come on, Sal; give me the Reader's Digest version of the story."

"It all happened so fast," I said. "When I think back on it I can't even remember the medical details. Anthony was born with a heart defect, they tried to fix it, and he died on the operating room table."

"That is the condensed version," Elaine said. "But it really doesn't all happen that fast, does it? The new life that you never wanted to live unfolded a lot slower, didn't it?"

I opened both of our straws and stuck them into the sodas, pushing Elaine's towards her, never once moving my stare from the center of her old, tired, hazel eyes.

"Why do you want to put me through this?" I asked.

"I need some background for your empty spaces column," she said. "I get to sit across from the great writer. I want the scoop."

"There's no easy way to step through grief," I said. "It's even worse when you try and match steps with someone else through it all. There's too much blame to go around. There's way too much anger, pain, and devastation. I was destroyed. Jenna was inconsolable. Our hearts were damaged. The heart that we shared was obliterated. As a couple we died right alongside Anthony on that table."

The liver spots on Elaine's hands came into clear view as she reached across the table to grasp my free hand. The familiar pain that was building in the delicate spot just behind my eyes blocked the sounds of the diner out.

"Did you hate her when she bailed on you?" Elaine asked.

"No, not at all," I answered a little too quickly. "I knew that she wasn't thinking right. She kept saying that I gave her a defective baby, but that was the pain talking."

"How did it end?" Elaine asked.

Despite the fact that we had shared a number of lunches we had never dug so deep into the life that Jenna and I once had. I was certain that Valerie had probably shared the story with her mother, but for some reason, with the threat of dying fresh in her mind, she wanted to hear it straight from my mouth.

"I came home from work one afternoon and Jenna was sitting in the exact position on the couch where I'd left her that morning. It didn't look like she moved even a muscle in ten hours. I knelt in front of her, grabbed her hands, and she started crying again. When her breathing got even she wiped her eyes and said, 'You should go.' That's the last time I ever saw her."

Randi returned to our tableside. She placed our plates in front of us and stood looking at Elaine with her hands on her hips. "Is there anything else you need?" she asked.

"You couldn't find that smile?" Elaine asked.

The smile materialized slowly, but when it showed itself the tension in their earlier encounter dissipated.

"There you go!" Elaine said. "You're such a pretty girl."

"I just hate working here," Randi said. "I can't wait to quit this job."

Elaine lifted her half a sandwich. The white cheese left a trail to the plate.

"That's the thing," she said. "I'm an old lady now. I used to spend my days waiting for my ship to come in. Now, I live in the moment. All I'm thinking about is spending time with my friend and eating this sandwich. I don't want to be anywhere else."

Randi laughed. She had no idea that what Elaine was telling her was life-affirming advice that would serve her well throughout her days. "That's 'cause you don't work here," Randi said. "If you did, you'd want to leave too!"

We watched Randi head to the next table.

"What an idiot," Elaine said. I watched Elaine's eyes close as she bit the sandwich and enjoyed the simple taste of it on her tongue. It looked so good I took a bite of my sandwich, and smiled.

A half an hour later I dropped Elaine back at her home. Before she stepped out of the car, she made a considerable effort to lean across the seat to kiss my left cheek. I tried to return the kiss, but she had deftly moved away.

"We aren't making out, here; I was just thanking you for sharing with me."

Elaine moved slowly up the walk, and I waited for her to open the front door and disappear into the house for her long afternoon nap. She didn't turn to watch me leave.

I headed back to my condo and checked the answering machine. The light was solid meaning that I didn't have a message waiting. I did have a dog waiting, however, and I made his day by opening the door for him so that he could race around to the passenger side of the car. I was filling an empty space by taking my dog for a drive around the neighborhood.

As Max settled into his seat, I turned on the classic rock station and backed out of the driveway. A Springsteen song blared through the speakers as I thought about my son. He was a beautiful boy that I never got to know.

Anthony was born with his heart valves all out of sorts. His aorta was displaced with the aortic and pulmonary valves connected to each other's corresponding arteries. There was a hole between the left and right ventricles, and the muscles of the right ventricle were too thick.

The man who was charged with putting Anthony's heart back together was a no-nonsense guy named John Elvin. There was an undeniable arrogance about Elvin, but I didn't much care if he treated me with respect. I just wanted him to fix our kid. Turns out, he couldn't, and he was fairly unapologetic about it as well.

"These things happen," he explained. "Sometimes there is too much a mess made of things. I did my best."

Jenna and I leaned on one another for support in that non-descript waiting room just off the OR. I hugged her close, and she trembled like a wounded bird against my chest, but just mere seconds later, she was free and running down the hall at Elvin who was walking slowly away, glancing down at a clipboard.

"You mother-fucker!" she screamed.

Jenna's rolling tackle took Elvin straight to the ground, and by the time I arrived on the scene she was sitting on his back, slapping at his balding head.

It took a month to talk the hospital out of pressing charges against Jenna. John Elvin has never once sent me a Christmas card, and despite wanting to reach out to him through the years, I have resisted the urge.

I drove down I-95 with Max's head hanging out the window. The afternoon air was crisp, but I had the heater on to keep me warm. What good is a ride in the car if you can't stick your head out the window? The Springsteen song gave way to a Van Halen guitar wail and I hummed along.

What could I possibly do about Valerie? If Jenna came barreling back into my life it wouldn't be fair to expect Valerie to sit idly by as I tended to Jenna's needs. I thought of what Valerie said about loving me more than anyone had ever loved me, but the problem was that I loved Jenna more than I loved anyone else, with the possible exception of the love that I held for my dead son.

I cried as David Lee Roth sang. Sometimes there was just no way to fill the empty spaces.

Jenna took New York by storm when she arrived. She started her acting career on a long-running soap opera playing a bitch of a woman who was more cunning than beautiful. The world took notice. It didn't even seem to me as if she were playing a part. I recognized some of the improvised lines that Jenna sprinkled through into her dialogue. The things that she said to me to make me fall in love with her were the very same lines that she used to capture the imagination of a waiting public.

Jenna's form graced the covers of all the men's magazines. She was careful to remain tasteful in her image, appearing in a bikini now and then, but always leaving something to the imagination. A film career was the natural steppingstone, and she played a love interest for Keeanu Reeves in a movie, but the acting was poor, the script was worse, and the critics were unmerciful. Jenna didn't seem to let it bother her, but we were no longer sharing the same breathing air and I was sure that she felt personally disrespected by the failure of the film.

All I knew of her now was what I saw on the television. Her engagement to Frank Powers, a trucking tycoon, was announced on Entertainment Tonight. I was unfortunate enough to have seen the interview live.

"All my life I've wanted children," Jenna gushed. "I can't wait to be a mommy!"

There was no mention of Anthony or me. It was as if we never even happened.

***

Twenty minutes later, with my mind centered only on the pain that living brings, Max and I arrived at Valerie's front door. Valerie's car was parked askew in the driveway as if she had been chased into the driveway. I figured that she was in a hurry to reach the bathroom as she always waited until the last possible moment before she took a pee. There really wasn't anything that I didn't know about Valerie, and as I rang the doorbell like an uninvited guest, it entered my mind that I did love her, but certainly not in the same way that I loved Jenna. Was it fair that I was even standing here?

Val opened the front door and the look on her face was a mix of relief and aggravation. "Taking the fleabag for a ride?" she asked.

"How'd you know?" I asked.

"I can set my watch by your life," she said. She leaned in and kissed my lips so quickly that I wondered if I imagined it.

We were just a few steps into the living room when she lowered the boom. "I'm thinking we should stop seeing each other for now," she said. Her voice broke and I heard the little guy in my head beg for me to keep her from crying.

"We can't pretend there's not an elephant in the room. I'd appreciate it if you can still visit with Mom and take her to her treatments, but if you can't, I understand."

I stopped walking, but Valerie continued into the kitchen and disappeared behind the solid wall adorned with photos of her mother and father from years gone by. I didn't follow her, mainly because I didn't want to see her cry.

"I'm not even sure what's going to happen," I said. "I haven't even spoken to Jenna. I may tell her that I can't help her."

Valerie reappeared from the kitchen. She was wiping her hands with a bright red dishtowel.

"We both know you won't do that," she said.

I made two quick steps towards her, but she dismissed me with a back wave of her hand.

"You better go," she cried. "Max is slobbering all over the inside of your truck."

The sound of the door closing behind me was deafening.

That night, I began work on the next column. The way that life was coming at me, I was going to be able to write about a years worth of material in about a week. I worked on it through the early evening, as Max snored on the floor beside me.

Everything I Know about Frustration

It certainly seems that I've spent a lot of time throughout the years seething about this or that. It's been a lifelong battle to gain emotional control over all kinds of silly little things, and the burning frustration is sometimes undeniably blinding.

There are a few things that I absolutely know for sure.

1). There are people and situations that I need to learn to live with and no amount of resistance will allow for accomplishment.

2). I'm supposed to be practicing peaceful thinking, but every time I try it I think of the Seinfeld episode where George's father is screaming "Serenity Now!"

3). There are people out there who try to compensate for their own failings by tearing you down. They will be forever ready to pounce.

Of course, people pay thousands and thousands of dollars every year to try to get on top of their own emotions. That seems a little crazy to me, so I've learned to practice a bit of mind control.

Be very warned - it doesn't always work, but lately, the urge to choke some poor unsuspecting man who had the gall to block the right turning lane when I needed to turn is lessened.

How do I accomplish this?

First off, learn to do all that you can do in a day. Stop. Do no more, and rest. We all want to be productive in all aspects of our lives. We want to compete to be the best we can be. Burning out doesn't allow that to happen. So rest a little.

Secondly, don't plot out the next day while you're trying to close your eyes. Read a little. Let the mind decompress. Ease out of the day. I have always had trouble sleeping and marvel at someone like my girlfriend who closes her eyes and starts snoring all in the same motion.

"Don't you have a thought in your head?" I asked her one morning.

"Nope, I just go to sleep."

It works.

Lastly, I have a saying that I've been repeating over and over to myself - sort of my own 'Serenity Now!'

In your patience you shall possess your soul.

Nice, huh? It's worked a couple of times, so I've tried it.

Relax, lesson muscle tension, flush the mind through a period of quiet, and repeat my phrase. The mind is a capable of blocking out any annoyance. You just have to determine if you really want to block it out.

That's Everything I Know about handling frustration.

I drifted off to sleep with the idea of handling frustration burning through my brain stem. At exactly four minutes after two, as a heavy rain pelted the bedroom window, and thunder rolled across the pitch-black sky, the ringing telephone rose above the noise.

CHAPTER 4

A full cup must be carried steadily.
English Proverb

"I'm going to kill the son-of-a-bitch!" Jenna screamed. Her words were slurred as though she'd just woken up from a spot in an alley somewhere after swilling wine with a homeless man.

"Calm down, Jenna, you're hurting my ear." I said.

Max danced in front of me, no doubt picking up on the sense of urgency in my tone.

"He took Tyler! He got an order of protection! I can't see my own son! He froze my fucking bank account! He threw me out on the street!"

I held the phone away from my ear. Every word was a chore, but with each sentence Jenna's voice rose until she sounded more like a monster than the beautiful woman that I had cherished and adored.

"Where are you?" I asked.

"New York!" she said. "I'm at a friend's apartment. Come and get me, Sal! Come and help me, please!"

Over the next twenty minutes, I was able to coax a partial story from Jenna. Her relationship with the powerful man was about what I suspected it might be, but it didn't bring me even a tiny bit of satisfaction. Good old Frank pulled a Tiger Woods on Jenna, hosting scores of women behind her back while pretending that he was the world's number on citizen.

"There's a condo about a block from his fucking office," Jenna screamed. "He pops out of a meeting, bangs a whore, and then goes to his next meeting!"

Remembering how Jenna had attacked the doctor, I wondered what had happened when she found out about the cheating. If one thing was certain it was that Jenna didn't take the news lying down.

"One of the sluts called the house wondering why Frank was running late. I mean, I sort of knew, but I didn't want to know. I pressured her a bit and she spilled the beans, saying that she was banging Frank for five years. So I went down to the office and caused a bit of a scene, I'm sorry to say."

"How bad was it?" I asked.

"A real doozy," Jenna laughed and cried all in a single sound. "I ran past his clueless secretary and kicked open the conference room door. There were about twelve people in there. I called him an asshole and threw a stapler at him. The secretary grabbed me. I kicked her legs out from under her and she hit the floor so hard I thought she'd go through it. All hell was breaking loose, of course, but I got my hands on a computer monitor and I smashed it through a mirror that was hanging on the wall. The company logo was emblazoned in the mirror. The glass was flying all over and every asshole in the room was rushing for cover."

In other words, she had handled it just as I thought she might. Chaos and frenzy were her operational modes and the passion in her voice as she retold the story captured my full attention.

"Security handcuffed me and escorted me to the street, but he didn't press charges. He just let me go. So, I drove straight to the school, but Tyler wasn't there. The principal said that she'd been instructed to tell me that Tyler was no longer my son."

Jenna's voice, which had vibrated my eardrums just moments before, was but a whisper now as she sobbed through the heartbreak of losing her son.

"He can't just take him away," I said.

"It's a different world than the one you live in," Jenna said. "He has so much money and I'm a television star. The reporters are lined up outside. The court papers have been filed. He's prepared for this battle and I'm not. I need you to get me, Sal. You're the only one who can keep me alive through this."

My mind clicked through the limited options available to me. I thought of Valerie and Elaine and Max. They were the ones who would be most affected by the next sentence that would leave my mouth. I had my own life now. Could I just up and leave them to help Jenna survive? Was my life about the love of the past or the future that I was trying to build? Was I ready for the pain of the past to shatter the calm of what I knew to be true? There really wasn't much of a decision to be made.

"I'll take the next plane out," I said. Jenna recited the address to her friend's home.

"Just hurry," she whispered. "'Cause I swear to God, if I lose another child, I'll kill myself."

The line went dead.

What choice did I have?

My next telephone call was even more unsettling.

"I need a favor," I said when Valerie came on the line.

There was no fooling her.

"You talked to her, didn't you?" Valerie asked. "I can tell that you did, you sound different."

"She's in trouble," I said. I led with the fact that Jenna had threatened suicide and explained all of it to Valerie leaving out the part about the handcuffs and the shattered mirror.

"And what do you need from me?" Valerie asked.

"I have to fly up there," I said. "I know this won't be easy, but can you keep an eye on Max for me? Feed him. Let him out a couple of times a day. I won't be gone much more than a couple of days."

The line was silent for so long that I had to ask if she had hung up.

"I'm here," Valerie said.

Still, she kept me hanging on.

I was on the verge of telling her about the afternoons that I'd spent with Elaine, waiting as she underwent treatment. In a game of one-upmanship I was about to show the only card that I had.

"Fine," she said. "Keep me posted on how your new relationship works out, would you?"

Valerie had a sing-song quality to her final question and the absurdity of it all played through my mind long after she clicked the phone off, allowing me the time to toss a few things in a bag and rush off to the airport.

The hurt and self-pity that had enveloped me in the years following Anthony's death threatened me once again as I rushed through the airport travel experience. As I parked the car in the long-term parking at BWI, I thought of how much time I'd put in regaining my own sense of worth. Jenna and I had erected our relationship on a foundation of mud and sticks and it had crumbled under our feet. How would I play in that mud again and not get dirty?

I tossed my small bag in the rack on the shuttle bus and listened to the small black man comment on the unseasonably warm weather. He was speaking about loving the springtime and the rebirth of it all. I had been reborn in my own mind, offering up pearls of wisdom to my readers on columns of paper that I was now threatening to burn. The outside temperatures were warming but I felt a freezing rain inside. I tipped the man a five, grabbed my bag and hustled across the street to the Southwest window.

As I checked my bag and paid double price for the round-trip ticket to New York, I was able to set all of my misgivings aside. I was certainly about to toss away all that was right in my life for the mess that was Jenna, but for the first time in so long I felt undeniably alive. I loosened the strings on my tennis shoes, undid my belt, and showed the man at security my identification. The muscle-bound, balding man examined my driver's license for a long moment to ensure that the man standing before him was the same man who posed for the photo. Physically I matched up, but if he could see through me, he would know for sure that I was a true fraud.

"Thank you, enjoy the flight," he said.

I nodded and gathered my belongings. 'Enjoy the flight'. There truly was little chance of that happening. There was a dirty wind blowing through my heart and mind. Jenna was like a full-force gale that would tear me asunder and leave me fighting for air. On some levels, I really wished that security guard had stopped me.

As the plane lifted off the ground, I scanned the area below the wings. For Jenna I would walk out on the wing of that moving airplane and try to grab hold of the clouds that hugged the plane. I would reach through, trying to grab a star that I could present to her on a soft white pillow. I would return Anthony to her, healthy and whole and ready to start life. I would offer her the sun and moon, and this time, she would accept it from me.

Not even knowing that I was tired, I closed my eyes and slipped into a troubled sleep that lasted nearly the entire flight. When I startled awake, the plane had started to descend. There was a spot of drool on my left shoulder and the poor young woman beside me repositioned herself to get as far away from me as possible. I thought of Valerie, and of Elaine. I thought of all of the days in my wake, and the healing that I had done.

It's all over now, I thought. *There's nothing to look forward to now but pain.*

I had just settled into the cab and repeated Jenna's address to a man who sported a heavy beard and a dark complexion, when my cell phone rang and one word flashed across the screen: 'Elaine'. I sighed and clicked the phone to life as the driver made a comment about the upscale neighborhood where Jenna's house stood.

"Good morning," I said.

"It's the middle of the afternoon, jackass," Elaine said. "I heard that you're in the middle of completely screwing up your life," she added.

"Great to hear from you," I said.

"I have your dog," Elaine said. "I'm not giving him back either unless you come to your senses."

Why did she have Max? What had Valerie done? Couldn't she just let the damn dog out and feed it for me?

"Whoa, why do you have Max?" I asked.

"Because you can't just walk out the door and just leave him high and dry because Jenna calls. Think of how much that dog will miss you! He'll wander around wondering why you abandoned him. He can't just understand that you have something else to do. He will simply wonder why his love and dedication were ignored because you found something better to do. He'll be hurt, can't you see that?"

I sighed heavily. Max was Valerie and Elaine. Max was the forgotten love, swept aside by a force that was too powerful to sidestep.

"I'm sorry," I said. "I'll be back shortly. Don't go all dramatic on me."

"Who's being dramatic?" Elaine asked. "Max will stop crying. He'll move on eventually and start thinking of other things. That's the way it works. People disappoint you and you learn to live with it."

The conversation wasn't going anywhere. Elaine was serving a purpose and all I could do was ride out the storm. I didn't want to give her the opportunity to make me feel guilty about missing her next doctor's appointment so I tried to shift the conversation.

"Max will be good company for you," I said. "I appreciate your help. Thank you."

"Anytime," Elaine said. She coughed violently before she could offer another smartass jab, she excused herself from the call saying that she needed to get some water. I said goodbye but I was talking to an abandoned line.

The cab driver whistled as we entered the wealthy section of town. Clean streets lined by large weeping willow trees. The homes were getting larger by the quarter mile. Long, winding driveways hidden behind big steel gates. The extravagance of life in the Hamptons was mocking everything about the poor, mundane existence of the man behind the steering wheel, as well as the man shifting uncomfortably in the backseat.

"Are you a movie star?" the man asked in what could best be described as broken English.

"Do I look like a movie star?" I asked.

The driver pulled the cab to the huge gate at Jenna's listed address before he could even formulate the 'what should I do' question the gate slid open and Jenna's voice came over the speakers. "Come on up," she said.

It was difficult to turn my eyes from the perfectly landscaped yard, and I'd never seen so many beautiful, different colored flowers. Red, gold, violet and blue. Each flower was already reaching for the sky despite the early season.

"Wow," the cab driver said. He was no doubt thinking about a massive tip. He had no idea that I wouldn't be able to provide it.

Jenna emerged from behind a huge wooden, black door. She was holding a martini glass in her right hand and a cigarette in her left. She bounded down the steps and met the driver at the door of the cab. She handed three one-hundred dollar bills to the man to pay the hundred dollar fare, and then she turned her attention to me.

Long after we watched the cab disappear out the front gate, we held our embrace. Jenna was crying softly into my shoulder as I took in every second of the moment. The scent of her hair; the softness of her touch; the sound of her cries; and the feel of her kiss on my lips all combined to bring the tears to the surface. I was exactly where I'd always longed to be, and we both knew it. At that precise moment I was certain that I would be ill-equipped to even pick Elaine, Valerie or Max out of a lineup. It was all about Jenna. It always had been.

"We'll get through this," I whispered as I fought off the tears.

"I'm glad to hear you say that," Jenna said. "Because it's just a matter of time before they come to arrest me. I smashed his car windows and flattened his tires."

"Why of course you did," I said.

Jenna hadn't aged even a little. She was still the beautiful-faced, elegant woman I'd met all those years ago.

"So beautiful," I whispered.

"Don't get all lovey-dovey," she said. "We have a lot of work to do."

I followed Jenna through a foyer that was as large as my entire apartment. Holding my hand for guidance, she brought me to a large sofa in a room that looked like it hadn't been sat in for years. Jenna's friend, Kayla, was also a soap opera star, and she had opened up her home for Jenna as soon as the shit hit the fan.

"You know what bothers me most about it?" Jenna whispered as we sat on the couch facing one another. Her martini glass was on the side table. Her sparkling eyes threatened tears, but she stared at me so long that I started to squirm under her glance.

I knew that I wasn't supposed to answer the question about what bothered her, but she hesitated for a long time.

"I love him," she said. "If he walked through the door I'd take him back, no questions asked."

"The heart wants what the heart wants," I said. The words sounded lame as they reached my own ears, but I thought of why I was sitting there as well. Why hadn't I just stayed home with Valerie?

Jenna's small hands were wrapped around my right hand. Her touch made me feel so alive, and I considered drawing her to me for an embrace, but she was lost in her own emotional battle.

"His lawyer called and said that they'd offer me a considerable sum of money if I'd just go away. He wants Tyler and he says that his son is better off without me. Can you imagine? I'm not losing another son."

Jenna's eyes filled with tears so quickly that I wondered if something was broke inside of her. A tear rolled down her right cheek and I followed its path to the couch. "I did that to you," Jenna said. "I walked away as if nothing ever happened."

I pulled Jenna to me. She sobbed into my shoulder, and I ran my hand through her golden hair. "We can work on me and you later," I whispered. "Let's work on you and Tyler first."

Jenna wiped the tears away. I recognized as a steely, defiant expression took hold.

"Naturally, I told the lawyer to go fuck himself."

"Naturally," I said.

"So what do I do? That's why you're here. You're going to tell me what steps to take."

"First off, you're going to have to stop acting emotionally," I said. "You're going to have to restrain yourself from attacking him physically."

Jenna smiled. Her facial expressions reminded me of the weather. Jenna could be all four seasons in a matter of minutes. The winds were blowing hard, and the thunder was rolling across her eyes.

"You need a lawyer," I said. "He's going to take the battle to the courts now, and he's on top of it all. You have to figure he's about eleven steps ahead of you, so you need to catch up a bit."

Jenna's resolve seemed to take a bit of a hit as she realized that I was most likely reading the situation perfectly. She reached for the martini glass, but I grabbed her hand instead.

"Drinking won't help," I said.

"Give me the fucking martini," she said.

I allowed her hand to reach the glass.

"All right, drink then, but it's going to stop you from thinking straight. He's thinking straight. He's doing his homework. You're throwing tantrums and swilling booze. Who's gonna' win that fight?"

Jenna took a healthy gulp, draining the glass, never once moving her eyes away from the hole that they were boring in my own eyes. She very calmly threw the glass off the wall behind the couch and it shattered into a few thousand splinters.

"Done drinking," she announced as she smiled. She moved forward and kissed me on the lips. "What else?"

"The first thing you need to do is figure out what you want. Say I give you three wishes, right now. What do you want?"

"First," she hesitated for a long moment, "I want another martini."

Her mischievous smile caused my heart to do a leap in my chest.

"After that, I have no idea." The smile gave way to tears once more. "I really don't have a fucking clue."

The worst part of it all was that I didn't have a clue either. I wasn't even sure what I wanted out of the situation. Was I really here to help her get her husband and child back? Weren't my intentions absolutely selfish?

"Does Kayla have a driver?" I asked.

"Of course, why?" Jenna asked.

"I asked you what you wanted and you said, 'another martini'," I said. "Let's go get one."

"But you said I shouldn't drink anymore."

"Once more," I said. "Let's get to the bottom of it all."

I was dead-set against taking Jenna to one of her high society drinking establishments. For one thing, we did not need to be planted in a situation where we were pretending to be something that we weren't. Secondly, Jenna had broken windows and slashed tires. I didn't want her running smack dab into someone who knew her or Frank.

"Where are we going?" Jenna asked.

We were side-by-side in the back of Kayla's Lincoln Navigator. I had asked the driver to find an Applebee's or a TGI Friday's and he had simply nodded.

Ten minutes later we were in the parking lot of a Mexican-themed drinking establishment called Cinco De Mayo.

"Does this work?" the driver asked.

"It's perfect, I can go for a margarita," Jenna said.

I followed Jenna to the table just off the bar. Every head in the room turned in her direction as we walked, and as usual, I felt honored to be the guy walking beside her. A young man in a Sombrero took our drink order.

"You know what amazes me?" Jenna asked.

A basket of tortilla chips with dipping sauces was placed between us as I pondered her unanswerable question.

"What amazes you?" I asked.

"How easy it is to fuck up your life," she said. "Life and love really should be easy, but it isn't, you know? Sometimes I lie in bed as the sun comes up, before anyone else is awake, and I think that if I just stay under the covers then nothing shitty can happen."

"There's a price we pay for being involved though," I said. "We all have the choice to be free of the love and the attachment, but we long for it, because the accumulation of such things is what living is about."

Jenna laughed. The sound of her laughter grew more audible as what I said sunk into her mind. "A fucking writer," she said. "I forgot you were so damn deep."

"It's my way of hiding," I said. "You break things and I think of things to make myself feel better."

Jenna stopped laughing abruptly as the sombrero-clad man set our drinks in front of us. The salt around the rim of the margarita was inviting and I raised my glass in a toast as Jenna's eyes found the tabletop.

"I try not to think of you and how much Anthony's death hurt you," she whispered. "At the beginning I used to read your column, but I stopped because I wanted to sweep it all under the rug. I'm sorry."

Jenna raised her glass. We tapped them together and sipped the drink. 'Bittersweet' was the word that entered my mind.

"Thank you for coming," she said. "I knew that you would."

"Grey skies or sunny days," I said. "When you left me I told you that you were priority one."

The awkward silence that took hold was making me undeniably uncomfortable so the next swig of my drink resulted in my draining nearly half the glass.

"To answer your question, though, I want him back."

I finished the rest of the margarita in the next gulp, and immediately ordered another.

***

Much later that night, as I tossed and turned in the guest bedroom, I cried for all that was lost in the storm of my life. Jenna was right. Life would be simple without the love and attachment. I considered calling Valerie and begging her to take me back, holes and all, but I didn't do it because she wasn't what I wanted. My heart desired the complete mess of a woman that was sound asleep two rooms away.

I struggled out of bed, grabbed my laptop and put together the weekly column. I e-mailed it to the paper. When I finished writing, I figured that it was just more useless motivational talk to a readership that most likely wouldn't do anything with my useless babble.

Everything I Know About Navigating the Choppy Waters

Someone once told me that I shouldn't make the losses of today turn into the enemy of tomorrow. It took me a long time to realize that carrying the pain from one day to the next, holding onto the grudges, and dwelling on disappointments wasn't doing much for me in setting the ship straight.

Thinking about your life as a ship out on the sea is an old trick. We know that we are supposed to ride out the storms, and head for the clear waters that will hopefully arrive and carry us to the next port.

Yet where on Earth is the pain of life greater than that of a tortured soul? The circumstances of life are not permanent even if they certainly seem that way. How is it possible to steer the ship back to the calm, clear waters where the sun can hit your face?

It's certainly true that failure and frustration are in the unwritten pages of everyone's record and that men don't break down because they are defeated, but because they believe they are.

It is essential to walk quietly around a dark situation as you search for a sliver of light. It's even more important to dream big, think big and act big. The storms will pass. You need to be big enough to withstand their force.

Never settle for less and remember how to dream big. Everything I know about calming the turmoil of an unsettled sea is going to come from deep below the surface.

Remember that faith and effort generate dynamic power.

At least that's what all the good books say and that's Everything I Know about surviving.

CHAPTER 5

*"A handful of patience is worth more
than a bushel of brains."*
Dutch Proverb

I turned in the bed and immediately jumped as I rubbed against
Jenna's naked frame. True to her nature, she didn't hear my response
at all. Jenna had always slept soundly and I thought about telling
her that she could sleep on the side of the road next to a four-
lane highway. The fact that she didn't hear my startled movement
allowed me the chance to feel the closeness of her body, smell the
fragrance of her skin, and examine her beautiful face. I only did this
for about twenty minutes as I wondered why she was torturing me
in such a manner. When had she arrived in the bed? What had she
been trying to achieve? I resisted all urges to reach under the covers,
but I certainly imagined us making love all through the day. It just
couldn't happen.

I pulled on a pair of red gym shorts and made my way to the
kitchen area. The house was quiet, and despite the fact that I had no
idea where anything was stored, I got a pot of coffee brewing and
retrieved the newspaper from the front stoop. I was halfway through

the editorial page when a loud knock on the door, followed by nine consecutive rings of the doorbell, nearly caused me to jump out of my skin.

"Don't answer it!" Jenna yelled. In seconds, she was before me, still naked, rubbing sleep from her eyes. "It's the fucking cops!" she added.

The fact that the police were at the door may have reminded me that I was facing more than I bargained for, but Jenna's perfect body was pushing those thoughts far from my mind.

"Stop drooling," she said. She made her way to the coffee pot as though everything was perfectly normal.

The knocking grew louder as one of the officers identified himself and shouted that he was indeed looking for Jenna.

"They showed up in the middle of the night," Jenna said. "That's why I climbed in bed with you. I hope you don't mind."

I couldn't think of a single thing to say in response.

Jenna poured the coffee and added French Vanilla creamer that she had to bend to find in the low shelf of the massive stainless steel refrigerator. Suffice to say that I watched every second of her movement.

"I'm going to go get dressed," she said. "Invite the officers in and tell them they are welcome to wait, but that I won't be rushed.

I thought of Max back at home, wondering where I'd run off to. If I were back in Baltimore he'd be beside me as I jogged through the park. Later I would stop at the store to buy a chew toy for him and an energy drink for me. Life would be so much easier.

Jenna brushed by on the way to the bedroom. She stopped for a moment to allow me a nice, long gander at her breasts, and then she leaned in and brushed my lips with hers. "I won't be long," she whispered.

As I opened the front door, a stray quote from Mark Twain flashed across my mind. *A man cannot be comfortable without his own approval.* Jenna was so comfortable in her own skin that it made me chuckle.

The two officers were not amused at had to wait. They announced the warrant for Jenna's arrest on the charges that she'd vandalized property. I extended my hand and broke the bad news that they were going to have to wait some more as Jenna got dressed for the occasion.

It was a scene out of a bad B-movie as I sat at the kitchen table sipping coffee, and eating pastries with two men who were about the same age as me. The blonde-haired, well-built cop introduced himself as Matt Michaels, and the shorter, paunchier man went by the name of Jim Liberta. They seemed to be perfectly reasonable men who were a little surprised to be in such a neighborhood with an arrest warrant for vandalism. They weren't in the least bit enamored of the fact that Jenna was an actress. In fact, it seemed to annoy them to no end.

"I hate people of privilege," was how Liberta put it. "In some ways it's easier to deal with the dregs of society. At least we don't have to worry about lawyers and wasting our time."

"What do you mean?" I asked.

"Well put it this way," Liberta said. "We have to sit here for an hour as she dresses as slowly as she possibly can, but we can't leave because we have instructions from the judge who issued the warrant. Ten minutes after she's booked, she'll be out, and to be honest not a damn thing will come of this. It's a colossal waste of everyone's time."

I honestly couldn't disagree with him. It seemed to be a waste of my time as well.

"I'm not supposed to be spouting off here," Liberta continued as he reached for a refill of his coffee cup, "but you seem like a reasonable guy." He glanced up at me as if he were looking for me to agree with him. "Rich people are the spoiled kids of the world. They just grow up thinking everyone should kow-tow to them, and we do."

Little did this guy know that my entire relationship with Jenna was based on my bending over backwards.

"And there's nothing there," Liberta said. "The more honest, real relationships are built on so many more things than what people drive, or how big their fucking house is. I don't know your relationship with this woman, but I'm betting that when she gets dressed up she looks dynamite. It's like a costume."

Liberta was getting dirty looks from his partner who passed the time by taking in all of the excesses of the home.

"Yeah, we all hate rich people," I said, "but given the choice, we'd live just like them if we could."

Jenna emerged from the back bedroom in full costume. She would have placed a tiara on her head if she could have. Liberta did everything but whistle as he took in the sight of her. Michaels met her in the hallway, and was halfway through reading Jenna her rights before my heart settled back in my chest. Jenna was absolutely breathtaking in a tight-fitting white dress that showed her perfect form. She wore sparkling diamond earrings and a short perfectly positioned gold chain with a dangling crucifix.

"Did you bring your handcuffs?" she asked Michaels.

"I beg your pardon?" Michaels asked.

Jenna moved to the front window. She looked out the blind and extended her wrists out.

"Please cuff me," she said. "The media hounds are out there and I need to make sure I get full mileage out of this."

"See what I mean?" Liberta asked.

I just bowed my head and laughed. It was going to be a hell of a ride. Whether Jenna was wearing a costume or not, I wasn't about to miss a second of it.

Jenna was booked and fingerprinted. There were three charges against her all the result of her rampage against Frank's property. I passed the time by chatting with Jenna's lawyer, and watching the media jockey for position. There was little doubt that Jenna would garner page one of the New York Post and the photo of her entering the jail, with her hands cuffed behind her back would sell plenty of papers.

I settled into a hard plastic chair in the back corner of a filthy room that was home to discarded newspapers and coffee cups. My plan was to stay clear of the fray, but one of the reporters caught on to me.

"Didn't you come in here with her?" the man asked. He was a stereotypical news reporter holding a small pad with a pen tucked in his right ear. I was surprised that he would still go about his business in such a manner. Where was his I-Pad? His breath reeked of coffee and nicotine, and his brown eyes moved wildly from side-to-side. He stood no more than five-feet-three inches, and each of his movements reminded me of what a weasel might look like as a man.

"Aren't you the ex-husband? Don't you write the column in Baltimore?"

As his questions reached my ears, I thought of all of the ramifications. How would Valerie and Elaine react if the tentacles of the story reached their life? Did my readers need to know that I was embroiled in something that was quickly becoming a major scandal?

"I don't know what you're talking about," I said to the man.

"You are!" the reporter cried out. "You're Sal Piseco. *Everything I Know*, right? You had the dead kid, didn't you?"

I rose from the chair as the little asshole took two steps back, which was a good idea for his safety, as his mention of Anthony as 'the dead kid' infuriated me.

"Are you the other man? Is there more to the story? Were you there when she smashed his property?"

It was amazing to me but the man's face displayed fear, but he continued to ask questions of me. I kept moving forward slowly and he kept backpedaling, screaming out questions.

"Do you love her? Will she be living with you when she gets out? How did the kid die?"

It was the second mention of Anthony that made me do it. I jumped at the reporter. I hit him with a jarring tackle that would have made Dick Butkus proud. I heard his body crunch underneath me as his pen rolled free of his ear and across the tile floor. He groaned loudly but before I could bring my fist to his face, I was ripped off of him by at least two police officers.

"I'm fucking suing, you piece of shit!" the reporter screamed.

The entire ordeal had surely escalated. I was half-pushed and half-pulled by the two cops who'd sipped coffee with me earlier in the day, down a long corridor. They were reading me my rights as I walked.

***

Three hours later Jenna and I were sitting in front of a couple of freshly poured margaritas. Jenna raised her glass high, and the smile that controlled her pretty face had me laughing as well.

"I can't believe you got arrested," she said. "Good old 'The-world-is-a-wonderful-place-Sal' is fingerprinted and photographed."

Jenna raised her glass and I clanked it with my own as salt flew from the rim.

"He brought Anthony into it," I said. "The son-of-a-bitch had the balls to talk about my son as if I had a hand in killing him."

Jenna was quiet for a long moment. "They are looking for a story," she said. Jenna sipped her drink and made a sour face. "If you want to get out of this, you can."

I thought about the life that I'd left behind. For one reason or another, the image of Valerie, sweet-dependable, loving Valerie, popped into my head.

"Don't you have a girlfriend?" Jenna asked as if she were reading my mind.

"No," I said. "Not really."

As soon as the words left my mouth, I regretted them. I had denied a love that a week ago was as real as any love that I'd felt in my life.

"Then let's get the hell out of here," Jenna said. "I don't have to be in court for two months. He's not going to let me see Tyler. Let's go to Baltimore and start all over. It'll be just you and me. What do you say?"

Thankfully, my cell phone rang, leaving the question there on the table beside our drinks. The name of my editor at the Sun was flashing back at me.

"Do you have one more column?" Paige asked.

"I'm kicking around an idea for something about being negative all the time," I said.

"Perfect!" Paige said, "Because we all just heard about your arrest. How's this for negative? We're suspending your column after this next submission. So, my friend, make it good."

I returned to the table. My face must have given me away.

"Bad news?" Jenna asked. Her glass was nearly empty and she smiled brightly as she placed a tortilla chip on her waiting tongue.

"I think I just lost my job," I said.

"Perfect," she responded. "It's going to be just you and me. No distractions."

That night, I wrote and submitted perhaps my last *Everything I Know* column.

Everything I Know About Being Negative

There are people who are living among us, pretending to be actually living. Instead, they are fighting themselves every step of the way. Think about it. Do you know someone who lives life every single day as if they are trapped in a poorly written drama?

"I don't feel good."

"The boss hates me."

"I can't catch a break."

"Isn't that just awful?"

Those people don't realize what a severe drain they are on the rest of us who are trying to battle through our own problems and keep our own heads above the rising tide.

Years ago, I worked with two men. One was a construction laborer, Cyrus, who hated the fact that he always seemed to get the most demeaning of tasks to complete. One day I walked by him as he was digging an excavation.

"Can you believe this crap?" Cy asked.

To me it seemed as if he were completing a task that was perfectly designed for his job description.

"They got me digging a ditch!"

"You're a laborer, Cy. Did you think they were going to ask you to balance the books?"

The second man set his clock so that he was leaving for lunch at exactly noon. He would sit in his car and eat his lunch, timing his return to his office so that he arrived back at his desk no sooner than one p.m. His watch was also set for five when an alarm would ring to tell him that it was time to go home. I recall needing him to stay an extra few minutes one day.

"I'm not giving them even one extra second of my time," he said.

"Why do you hate life so much?" I asked him.

"Because it sucks," he answered.

I recently read of this man's passing. I could only think that he kicked and screamed until they closed the lid on his casket.

"You bring your own sunshine to the picnic," someone once told me.

*As Pollyanna as that seems it beats the crap out of always being miserable.
That is Everything I Know about being negative.*

After writing the column, I decided that another night at Kayla's
home, alone with Jenna, wasn't going to work for me. I stepped into
the living room and caught of glimpse of Jenna asleep on the long,
brown couch. Her body was safely hidden beneath a blue and white
throw blanket. The sounds coming from the television were that
of an informational about something that chopped onions. Jenna's
breathing was even, but every so often she'd offer a loud snore that
was so familiar to my ears. Looking at her resting my heart was filled
with a sense of wonder. How had we arrived at this place and time?
What would happen from here? Did she still love Frank? If she ran
off to Baltimore with me how would she find peace with Tyler out
of her everyday life?

"It's not going to work," I whispered to the man on the infomercial
who was so excited by how fast he'd chopped the onion.

I sat at the kitchen table with a blue ballpoint pen. I wrote the
note quickly.

*Hey Babe, heading back to Baltimore. Not walking out, but you
need time to think about what you want to do. If you still want to
come down, I'll pick you up the airport. You know I'd never leave you
hanging. I love you as much as I did on the day we were married, but
there's so much to consider. You need to find out about Tyler. Call me as
soon as you read this. Sal.*

Four hours later as the plane lifted off and broke through the heavy
clouds; I considered the fact that answering her call had thrown my
life into absolute chaos. I had been arrested for the first time in my
life. My column was about to go on hiatus. Valerie hadn't spoken

to me, and Elaine and Max were anxiously awaiting my first step through the door. I fell asleep with my head against the hard plastic beside the small window. The shade was still up. The view of life on the ground obscured by the heavy clouds. It wouldn't take long for me to break back through the clouds once we made our descent, but I had no way of knowing the chaos that awaited me on the ground.

CHAPTER 6

*"You can know what's in your life when you know
what's in your heart."*
Sam Keen

Sometimes I really hate my cell phone. That fact was never more evident than at the very moment when the announcement came over the speaker that it was okay to turn on our devices as we taxied to the gate. I clicked the phone to life and found that there were seven messages waiting for my response. Six of the messages were from Jenna. The other was from Valerie. I could almost guess the frantic tone that Jenna's messages would take on. I mindlessly decided that I needed to hear Valerie's voice first.

"We need to talk," Valerie said.

There was certainly no hint of love or hate in her message. Selfishly I thought of Max. Was Elaine okay? Was this about the arrest? Before I could even punch in the first number to return her call the phone rang. The number wasn't recognizable.

"Sal?" the voice was loud and angry in my ear.

"Yes, how can I help you?"

"Stay the fuck out of my life," the man said. "This is Frank Powers.

Stay the fuck out."

The line went dead. The message had been clear. The goddamn phone rang again.

"I'm pregnant," Valerie said. "I don't want anything from you, but I'm definitely pregnant."

She too, hung up, and just like that, everything I knew was completely out the window.

I dropped the phone to the floor of the plane and I deftly ground it into a mash of wires and plastic under the weight of my right heel. The woman seated across the aisle from me held a wide-eyed look of utter amazement.

"I was thinking of getting a new phone," I said.

***

I was so out of sorts that by the time I left the plane I was hyperventilating. The same woman who had watched me grind my phone to powder tapped me on the shoulder as we exited to remind me that I may have left my carry-on bag under my seat. I headed back to the plane and the attendant, a middle-aged woman that used to be very pretty, smiled at me as I returned.

"Did you lose something?" she asked.

"Pretty much everything," I answered.

I grabbed my bag and headed back through the plane door. The attendant returned to cleaning up the mess of magazine and drink cups left behind by the travelers. I had my own mess to tackle.

True to my nature, I decided to let a moment pass. Thankfully, I had smashed my phone so I wasn't tempted to just punch in numbers and react to what had happened. Frank Powers threatened me. Valerie was pregnant! Jenna was doing God knows what to further throw us into turmoil, and Valerie was pregnant!

I sat on a window ledge in front of a gate where a bunch of bored travelers were looking to head to Atlanta. The speakers crackled overhead but I didn't hear a word the woman was saying. A collective groan told me that the flight may have been delayed. My breathing evened out and I felt more aware of where I was than at any other time in my life. The sounds of a U2 song took hold. *With or Without You*, I believe. Bono sang out about reaching the shore through the storms.

The shore seemed miles and miles away.

Twenty minutes later, I finally arrived at my car. During the walk from the terminal to the parking lot, I imagined what my life would suddenly become. As I considered having a child, it was Anthony that I pictured in my mind's eye. Unfortunately, Valerie wasn't the one standing beside me. Gazing at the wonder of the newborn child, and holding tightly to my hand was Jenna.

I slipped in beside the wheel and started the car. Where the hell was I going? Valerie would be at work. Elaine's next appointment wasn't until tomorrow. Should I try and see if I could get my job back? A call had to be made to Jenna to see if she was still planning on playing house with me. Should I head off for a replacement phone?

I finally decided on the most prudent of all options. I needed to pick up my dog and go for a run. I thought of a column I'd written just months before. I had told my readers to meet the storm head on, and to stay balanced and clear-headed.

"What a bunch of shit!" I yelled out as I slammed my right hand off the steering column. For thousands of years, man after man, all better men than me, had tried to figure life out. I turned on the stereo to drown out the sounds of my own voice. Coincidentally it was U2 song: *Sunday Bloody Sunday*.

As I drove, I watched the storm clouds gathering through the side window of my truck. The sun was completely out-of-view by the time I hit I-95 on my way to Valerie's home. I kept glancing up to gauge the strength of the coming storm, but it was too difficult to measure. There was a chance that it might just all blow right on by. As the thought entered my mind, a clap of thunder roared and lightning brightened the sky. It was certainly heading right at me.

I pulled into Valerie's driveway. I was able to move right up close to the front door because Valerie's car wasn't in the drive. Her newspaper was on the front porch though and it was in danger of being battered by the rain, so I got out of the car with the mindset to place it in the front door. The front page flashed my press photo right back to me: *Columnist on Hiatus*, the article stated.

What does one do on hiatus? I certainly was taking a break about telling others how to live their life and respond to pain. I thought about leaving a note on the door, but what does one say in such a note? So glad you're carrying my child, but I'm not sure I love you?

I instinctively reached for the phone that wasn't there.

Someone had once told me that the way to make God laugh was to tell Him what you had planned. There was a certain truth to that. I slammed the car into reverse and hit the road aiming for Elaine's house. The sky opened up and the rain came down with a vengeance.

Pulling into Elaine's drive, I noticed that the rain had slowed to a barely perceptible drizzle. The door opened suddenly and Max came charging out and met me at the driver's side door. I bent to rub his ears, but he was by me and into the truck, panting excitedly, and begging me to get in and drive him away. Elaine was on the front porch, the door barely open, with a cane in her right hand. She was still in her pajamas, and even at a distance, I recognized a sarcastic smile.

"Hey fuck-up," she called out. "How's life treating you?"

I laughed as I bridged the gap between us. She still seemed to be on my side.

"Val's pregnant," I said.

"You think I didn't know that?" Elaine said. She disappeared behind the door, and by the time, I entered the house she was already on the couch. I shut the door as another rumble of thunder rolled across the sky. I couldn't stay long. Max would tear a hole through the roof of my truck if I did.

"Where's your wife?" Elaine asked.

"Jenna isn't here...yet," I said.

"That's a mistake, you know?" Elaine said.

Elaine settled on the couch under a Baltimore Ravens throw blanket.

"As it turns out, I know very little," I said. I sat on the edge of the couch across from Elaine's leather armchair. The sound of her laughter muffled the thunderclap above the house.

"That's not true," she said. "Actually we all know how to live life right. Sometimes we are just too weak to pull it off. The truly lost souls are the ones who cave into pressure, and just give up."

She was right. We both knew it.

"You ain't completely screwed yet," she said. "Keep it moving forward. You know what has to be done. I'm just interested in seeing if you can pull it off."

The rain pounded the driveway and we both concentrated on the sound of it. Once more, I thought of Max and how anxious he would be if I didn't get back to him.

"Take old flea bag home," she said. "The rain isn't going to let you get your run in. We have a chemo visit tomorrow that I can hardly wait for."

Elaine sipped from a half-empty mug of tea.

"Do you need anything?" I asked. "More tea?"

"It's half-full," she said. "Get the hell out of here, I'm tired."

Half-empty, half-full, we had agreed to disagree. I leaned in and kissed Elaine's left cheek. She smelled of sickness. The scent wasn't distinct to anything else I'd ever smelled, but it overpowered the tea.

"I can't wait to meet my grandchild," she said. "I just hope she's not here before the wedding, or before I buy the farm."

"She?" I asked, ignoring everything else in the sentence.

"Little Elaine!" she said. "We all get to dream!"

I wanted to kiss her again. She had made me feel as if it could all work out.

"Get the hell out of here," she said. "I'm tired."

I laughed as I ran through the raindrops to my waiting car. When I sat down in the driver's seat, Max licked the side of my face and settled in to see how I handled the trip home. Perhaps, there were a few things I still did know.

An hour later, I stood under the water in my shower. Max and I had torn through the rain, completing a jog that left me exhausted and soaked to the bone. Still I felt a little better.

The message light on my answering machine was blinking. The phone rang as I toweled off. The ringing stopped and then started again just a moment later. A simple thought crossed my mind.

Life doesn't have to be difficult.

As I dressed, I wondered about the validity of such a thought. Was it possible to live a full life without horrific pain? The telephone rang again. The voice was muffled by the bedroom door. I dressed slowly, considering how much we had grieved Anthony's death. We weren't the same people. The love we felt for one another had been rendered useless. Our awkward attempts to step forward sent us reeling into relationships that failed to satisfy our new partners. Jenna's life with Frank was none of my business now.

"Valerie's pregnant," I said to my bedroom walls. Max's ears perked for a split-second, but he settled back into the rug.

I knew the way out.

Or at least I thought I did before I listened to the answering machine messages.

There were thirteen messages. I listened to them in the order that they arrived. The first seven messages were from Jenna and her maniacal messages expressed every emotion in the rainbow of human experience. She explained that she needed me, that she loved me, that she now hated Frank and wanted him dead, and that she longed to be by my side. Every shriek of her voice drove me to the brink of insanity and back again. Message eight was from Valerie. It was her 'we need to talk' message. Message nine was a long political message that I erased. It was the only message that I erased along the line.

The tenth message was from my bosses at the newspaper wondering if I would like to discuss the suspension. It was followed by a quick confirmation of the chemo visit by Elaine, and the dentist called to confirm my appointment for later in the week. I was nearly through the messages. There was just one more.

"This message is for Sal Piseco. This is Thomas Reynolds of the *New York Post*. I am calling you to get your thoughts on this morning's murder of Frank Powers. Please return my call at your earliest convenience."

"WHAT?" I screamed the word so loud that Max jumped up from his spot on the floor.

I replayed the message. It was simple and direct and there weren't any hints or allegations. My mind went numb. Sweat presented itself on my forehead and under my arms. Did she kill him? The message had been left when I was drying off. The news of the murder was fresh.

Where was Jenna?

I scrambled for the phone, patting my pockets, again, for the cell phone that wasn't there. I grabbed the portable from its cradle and dialed Jenna's number. It went straight to voice mail.

"Call me!" I screamed.

I wasn't about to ask her any questions on the cell line.

What could I possibly say?

"My flight was good. Max says 'hello'. Did you murder Frank?"

I slammed the phone down a bit too hard. I didn't need to shatter it just then. It was my only form of communication.

Or was it?

For the next thirty minutes, I tried to reach Jenna every way humanly possible. I friended her on Facebook. I Google searched for her. I was a body frozen and a will that was paralyzed by fear. The house phone didn't ring, and if my cell phone was ringing it wouldn't be answered.

I also read the account of the breaking news story of the murder of accomplished businessman Frank Powers. The *Post* was reporting that Powers had been felled by a single shot from a .22 caliber pistol. There was little in the way of speculation, a first for a *Post* story, but Jenna's name was mentioned…and so was mine.

Police are in the process of investigating the shooting and have named renowned newspaper columnist Sal Piseco as a person of interest.

"I'm right here!" I announced to my bedroom walls, and just then Max ran to the front door. Three loud knocks followed.

They'd found me.

CHAPTER 7

After I'm gone I'd rather have people ask why I have no monument than why I have one."
Cato the Elder

I remember being a small child and seeing my first police officer at close range. The man had been directing traffic at church. Evidently, he knew my mother. As a little boy, I felt truly intimidated. Back then I was drawn of course, to the gun that was hanging on the officer's hip. All those days ago, the cop tousled my hair and grinned at my mother. "Someone is afraid of the cops," he said.

I felt the exact same way when I opened the door to the two men standing before me.

"Sal Piseco?" the tall, black man asked me.

My eyes went straight to the gun.

"How can I help you?" I asked.

The shorter, white cop, who also had a gun answered for him.

"We've been asked to stop by to see if you'd accompany us to the station to speak with a detective about a murder up in New York. Have you been to New York recently?"

By the way he framed the question there was no way to answer it in a manner that wouldn't make me sound guilty. The truth would set me free however and I swallowed my fear of the big guns on their hips and told the truth.

"I just got back today," I said. "Are you arresting me?"

The black man laughed. It was certainly a strange reaction. "Should we be?" he asked. "It'd make it a lot easier if you confessed off of one question, though."

Max was at my right leg. He was being awful quiet given the fact that there were two men standing in our doorway. Perhaps he had also noticed the guns.

"I'm just trying to figure out the semantics here," I said. "I write a newspaper column and sooner or later there's going to be a truck with a camera here and my neighbors are probably falling out their windows to see what the hell is happening. I certainly don't feel like riding to the station in the back of your car, and I guess I'm a little concerned about who will be questioning me. Are you the officers on the case?"

The black man's nametag told me that he was Cunningham. When my eyes went to it, the shorter guy turned to make his tag clear: Wilson.

"So what will it be officers Cunningham and Wilson? Can I meet with you, or whoever, at the station?"

Cunningham was nodding along with me. "Certainly," he said. "We were just sent out here to make sure you don't disappear until your name can be cleared. I read your column all the time, by the way. You've helped me through a lot of hard times."

"Excellent," I said. "Give me ten minutes and we can head down together."

The experts in life say that there is no such thing as a coincidence. I'm not quite sure who those experts are, but if that is true then what happened next is rather creepy. The telephone rang. Cunningham and Wilson had the same exact thought at the precise moment that I was thinking that I should shut the door on them and not allow them to hear the voice message that was about to shatter the awkward silence. They certainly wanted to hear the message. Jenna's hysterical voice filled the room.

"He's dead! The son-of-a-bitch is dead!"

Just then, the white van with the number seven in red lettering screeched to a halt. Max barked. Cunningham and Wilson seemed to reconsider their position as one of their walkie-talkies squawked.

"Any chance that you didn't make out that message?" I asked.

"Everything you know is sort of out the window right now, isn't it?" Wilson asked. "Maybe it would be better if you rode downtown with us."

"Let's go," I said.

"Would it be possible to grab your message tape?" Cunningham asked.

"Get a warrant," I said.

Wilson laughed. "Being a cop is a lot harder now that everyone knows their rights from watching television."

"I don't have anything to hide," I said.

I honestly hoped that were true. I patted Max on the head and closed the door before the fucking phone rang again.

The obnoxiously pretty blonde weekend reporter ran towards me with her microphone shaking. The cameraman was getting shots of my house from all angles with the small camera on his left shoulder.

My neighbors were standing in their front yards. Cunningham told me to watch my head as I slipped into the backseat of the police car. I didn't even hear the questions that the pretty reporter was shouting. I had run into her one time at a media cocktail party. She'd been so drunk then that I doubted she even remembered meeting me. Wilson backed the car out of the drive. Like every other man I'd seen as footage on the local news, I dropped my head away from the camera. I was innocent, of course, but if I were on the other end of the television screen, there'd be one word on my mind: guilty.

Of course, the television crews were waiting for us at the station. Cunningham and Wilson were gracious. They cleared a path for me, and kept the reporters at bay.

"WHERE'S JENNA?"

"DID YOU DO IT?"

"DID SHE DO IT?"

I couldn't answer the questions, but if I could the answers might be, 'I don't know,' 'no,' and 'she might have.'

My mind clicked through my options. Powers had called me to threaten me after I had left New York, so I didn't kill him. Yet, if I handed over that information on the answering machine tape, I would also have to give up the fact that Jenna wished Frank dead just moments later, and that she was still in New York for all I knew. Besides, I had crushed my phone with Frank's voice on it.

I needed a lawyer.

"It's actually turning into a nice day," Cunningham said. The rain and clouds had given way to a sun that was trying its best to brighten the sky.

"For most of us," Wilson said.

We arrived at the station door. Cunningham was my lead blocker, and Wilson protected by blindside. The long, dark corridor that stretched before me was a bustle of activity. The reporters and the cameramen were left out on the front step, but there were other officers and a few civilians hurrying by. My eyes found two very important people almost at a single glance. Standing on the right side of the hallway with her back pressed firmly against the wall was my pregnant girlfriend. We locked eyes for a split-second, and then she turned away, running from me, heading for the door and the open air. Thirty feet in front of her, on the same side of the aisle, there were two more officers struggling to get a hold of a combatant. Jenna was in full voice.

"Get your hands off me, you bastards!" she screamed.

I was directed to a room on the right side of the hall just as she was pulled across the threshold of a room on the left. I saw her and she saw me, and that's exactly what the officers had wanted to happen. Cunningham looked in my eyes, trying his very best to gauge my reaction. I didn't give away the thought that I was fairly sure that I was screwed.

I was led to a grey folding chair that had a fold in the right side as if it had once been thrown against the wall. There was a stained brown table in front of me and I leaned on my elbows and rubbed my eyes with the palms of my hand. Cunningham excused himself, asking me if I'd like a coffee for our chat. I told him that I liked a lot of cream and no sugar. Then I waited. For ten minutes, I sat alone.

How had they captured Jenna? When had she made her trip to Baltimore? What had she done in the time that I left her alone? There was no disputing the fact that Frank was dead, but had she even been there when it happened? Why had I thrashed my phone? If I hadn't, I might understand what I was up against, but Cunningham, or whoever was about to talk to me, certainly knew more about what happened than I did.

The room was certainly nondescript. There wasn't anything to look at other than the light green walls and the stained ceiling tiles. Was I being left to wait so that they could see how I'd react? Had I seen too many cop shows? Guessing along wasn't doing me much good. I made sure to breathe calm and easy, and the passing time allowed me to gather a bit of steam. I didn't have anything to do with a murder. I was pretty sure that Jenna wouldn't do it either. It would all go just fine, thank-you very much. By the time the door creaked open and Cunningham flopped in the chair across from me I was feeling pretty confident. I was blown out of the water by the first sentence out of Cunningham's mouth.

"Jenna is in there confessing to the shooting," he said. "She is telling everyone involved that it was your idea so that you two could be together again."

I searched Cunningham's dark face for even a hint of a smile. His nose seemed to be too big for his face. His mouth held a grimace and nothing more. He repeated his statement once more.

"Bullshit," I said after careful deliberation. "Jenna didn't shoot anyone and I certainly didn't plan it for her."

Cunningham waited a long time. He stared straight into my eyes as though he were trying to figure out if I was lying or not. It reminded me of the staring contests that you'd have with a classmate back in high school. I waited for his response, but there wasn't anything forthcoming. He nudged the cup of coffee towards me and pushed back in the chair. The sounds of the scrapping feet echoed through the empty room. He pulled the door closed as he left.

I picked up the coffee cup. There were images of playing cards around the body of the cup. I had a pair of aces and a pair of jacks sandwiched by an unturned card. A small note referred me to the bottom of the cup to see if I had completed the full house. How could I not look?

Three of hearts.

I hoped that it wasn't an omen. I sipped the coffee. It was like drinking dirty water. Cunningham returned in the middle of my second sip.

"All right," he said, as he placed a yellow notebook on the table in front of him. "Tell me what happened over the last few days."

I started with the first frantic phone call from Jenna and finished, twenty-five minutes later, with the recall of when he'd knocked on my door just an hour ago. Cunningham didn't react very much as I worked my way through it, showing only one sign of disbelief by shaking his head when I mentioned how I had ground my phone to powder on the plane.

"While you were out drinking with her did she intimate that she wished him dead?"

It was a fair question, of course.

"No, as a matter of fact, she told me that she loved him and that she wanted him back."

Cunningham nodded. He scratched notes on the pad, and then made a move to get up again. I imagined another long wait as he went over his notes with whoever was interviewing Jenna in the next room.

"You're free to go," he said.

"That's it?"

Cunningham picked up my half-empty coffee cup. "Your story adds up so far," he said. "But now we have to do our work. We have a dead body. It's not just going to go away, but so far...."

Cunningham's voice trailed off. Once more, he looked deep into my eyes as if he could perform some sort of medieval mind-read.

"We do have a warrant to search your property, of course, and if you can point us in the direction of your 'shattered' cell phone, we'd appreciate that."

He had made air quotes when he said the word 'shattered.'

"Certainly," I said.

What was the decorum when you parted ways with a man that had been interviewing you about a murder? Was I supposed to shake hands?

Cunningham answered the question for me. He disappeared through the door leaving me to follow his wake.

"I can't tell you what to do," he said, "but you might want to distance yourself from your ex-wife for the time being. She's certainly a firecracker, that one."

I'd once written a column about killing worry and rising above the sounds of one's own mind. If I still had my newspaper column it would be the column that I'd rewrite in the face of what I was facing.

I left the station through the front door, shrugging beyond the reporters and their questions. I turned right on Mission Street and broke into a slow jog that took me down the sidewalk of the city streets to the bus stop. My idea was to jump on the bus and head to Valerie's home, but I shifted gears, running faster by the stop, and down the bustling street. The words of the long-ago published column filled my mind as I ran. I didn't think of Jenna or Frank, or Elaine, or even Max. I simply ran. One foot in front of the other, worry disappearing from my mind as though there was nothing between me and freedom but the sound of my own breathing.

Everything I Know about Worry

Faith and fear are two of the greatest forces known to men, and in an ideal world, faith is stronger than fear. In the real world, it is usually the other way around. Worry is the by-product of fear and its meaning is rooted in the idea of being choked or strangled. We have all been choked by worry. Our minds very often take hold of a single thought or obsesses over an idea, strangling us of our ability to see clear to the other side.

I believe that it was Ralph Waldo Emerson who once said that if you 'Do the thing you fear then the death of fear is certain.' Smart man, that Emerson, because as I have made my way through this world, I have realized that when a man makes up his mind that there is nothing that he cannot endure, his fears will leave him. We are built to endure all the pain and discomfort that this world can muster. The trick is seeing clear through the fog to the clarity of the wide-open world on the other side.

There are times in the life of the mountain climber when he realizes that he can longer go down to protect his life, and at that moment he understands that the only way he can go is up. The mountain climber can certainly brood and worry about his predicament, but worry is a rocking chair that never takes you anywhere. Be bold as you break through the light of truth that breaks the fog of fear that is created in the walls of your own mind.

See your fears for what they are, stand up strong, and whip the very essence of fear. Your life may depend on it.

CHAPTER 8

"A kiss may ruin a human life." Oscar Wilde

For all of the aggravation that comes with having a cell phone I knew that I couldn't go without one much longer as my life spiraled out of control. I swung by the house just long enough to pick up Max, and together we made the trek to the Verizon store. All the while, I tried hard to take stock in where I was at the present moment. I was tired, hungry, awaiting a court date for assault, and a man-of-interest in a murder trial. I also hadn't yet spoken with the future mother of my unborn child, and I was still very much in love with my ex-wife, the mother of my deceased child.

I laughed. The famous writer of the spiritual column carried by hundreds of newspapers had authored such an existence.

For all of my recent incompetence I had done one smart thing over the last few months. I had purchased the insurance on the phone, and I explained what had happened to a ridiculously young and beautiful dark-haired girl at the technical assistance counter. She was in a bright red frock that was cut low to show her young breasts. I was pissed at myself for even looking, but they were right there in front of me. She smiled wonderfully and pointed me in the direction of my model of phone. Technology had made a number of advances since the last time I'd been in the store and I was in line for an upgrade if I wanted it.

"I really just want my old number back so I can check my messages," I said.

"That's not a problem," the girl said. She was looking down at a computer monitor that was built into the desk in front of her. Her elegant fingers moved quickly as she brought my account up on the screen. She glanced at the wall clock that was positioned on the far wall over my head.

"Time is moving so slow today," she said. "Fifteen more minutes and I'm out of here."

"Don't wish time away," I said. It was my natural response, but she simply shrugged and laughed it off.

"I'll gladly give up these last fifteen minutes. Working until seven on a Sunday night isn't my idea of fun."

Her mention of the day of the week reminded me that Elaine would be waiting for me to pick her up for her chemo appointment in the morning. I needed to see Valerie and work out some sort of understanding before Elaine plopped down in my passenger seat or I was in huge trouble. She would skewer me with her sarcasm.

Thankfully, the clerk was in a hurry because within five minutes I was back in my truck with my new phone powering up. Max was at my right shoulder. I hit the code to retrieve my messages, and listened as they played one after another.

Frank Powers had called me again. The warning about staying out of his life, repeated in an even more threatening tone. I wondered how soon after had he died. My heart sunk further in my chest when I listened to the six straight messages from Jenna. From what I could piece together, she booked the flight for Baltimore, but made one last ditch effort to wrestle her son away from Frank. She had certainly showed up at the gates of their mansion. A short time later, Frank was dead.

My second major problem was also chronicled in the confines of my saved messages. My editor, John Paige, had called and asked me to report to his office sometime in the morning. He made reference to the fact that not returning his call could result in serious consequences.

"Get in line," I said.

Valerie's messages were less threatening, but there was most assuredly a tone of great defeat, that she was not trying to hide. She didn't need me to feel as if I owed her a thing. She understood that life often doesn't work out as planned. Her unborn child would be her focal point now. There wasn't time left to fight for me.

Max was panting at the side window. He was a little confused that we weren't moving, but his mind seemed at ease as he watched the pedestrian traffic at the strip mall. We were still sitting in our spot when the young girl emerged from the front entrance of the store. She was excited to finally be free of her day of work. Max followed her skip down the sidewalk where she jumped into a waiting car filled with other over-anxious teenager types. Her whole life was in front of her.

"Time will mess you up bad," I said as I put the truck in reverse and backed out of the spot. An old Stones song blared from my speakers, <u>Happy</u>, with Keith singing, *I need your love to keep me happy, baby, keep me happy.*

It was time to straighten out a few things.

Over the course of the last year or so Valerie would head into the office on Sunday afternoon. She worked for a team of lawyers called Green, Babbitt and Feinstein. She enjoyed the challenges of the job, and loved the law. She was the executive secretary of the group and she took her job seriously. Her Sunday trips to the office would allow her to get a jump on what the partners needed to do during the week. Each week we would battle about her leaving the comforts of home to be at work, but I never once won the argument. Valerie was the opposite of Jenna in nearly every single way.

Max's hair was all over the passenger seat of the truck. His massive head hung out the side window as I drove down I-95 to the bullshit lawyer's offices. The parking lot was empty except for Valerie's white Honda parked in her usual spot. I eased in beside it, and looked around at the perfectly landscaped grounds and the huge fishpond that was off to the left side of the door.

"Chasing ambulances and preying on the hopeless and helpless pays," I said to Max. I patted his head and made sure his window was closed enough so that he wouldn't jump out and capture a fish or two. I never even made it out of the truck. Valerie opened the front door, and stood in place, waiting for me to arrive. I read the expression on her face from my spot behind the windshield. She was annoyed.

"What?" she asked as I made my way to her.

She was wearing a loose-fitting white sweater and a pair of dark jeans. I saw the small silver crucifix dangling outside her sweater, and her hands went to it, turning it nervously.

"I love you," I said.

I immediately wanted to snatch the words back before they had the chance to reach her ears. The look of annoyance, replaced by a countenance of utter amusement.

"Are you kidding?" she asked. Her eyes went to Max who barked his greeting.

"Can we take a walk?" I asked.

"Old fleabag coming?" she asked.

"Just me and you," I said. I stood before her, extending my arms out, wondering if she'd accept my hug.

"Come on, Mommy," I said.

Valerie stepped into the hug. After all, that I'd been through in the last 24 hours, I'm not going to lie, it felt pretty damn good.

Until she cried, that is.

We held the embrace in front of the fishpond as Max serenaded us with a chorus of healthy barking.

The lawyer's offices were part of a huge complex of buildings that proclaimed itself the business center of Baltimore. We headed away from the office on the perfect sidewalk, and Valerie walked slowly with her arms wrapped tightly to her body. I wanted to take her hand in a show of solidarity, but she wasn't offering it.

"First off, I love the fact that you're pregnant. Our baby is going to be so beautiful, just like you."

Valerie took eleven steps before she answered. I know. I counted them.

"Like I said before, 'Are you kidding me?' I called to tell you I was pregnant. I texted you. I e-mailed you. I did everything but send you a singing telegram and this is how you present it to me?"

"I lost my phone," I said. "I was arrested once for assault and questioned at length about a murder. I didn't have a lot of time to get back to you."

Valerie laughed.

Then she cried.

"I messed the whole thing up," she said. "I had a dream of how my life was going to play out and I really screwed it up."

I reached for her, but she spun out of the way.

"How about Jenna?" she asked. "Where is she? I know she's here. I saw her at the police station."

"She *is* here," I said. "But I don't know where."

Max was barking again. I glanced back at the car and saw that a running squirrel was the reason for Max's discontent. It dawned on me that it would be so much easier to be a dog.

"She's not at your place?"

"She might be," I said. "But I'm here with you."

Valerie resumed walking at a much brisker pace. I actually had to jog to catch up. Once more, I resisted the urge to put a hand on her.

"You saw her. Did you sleep with her? I don't even care!"

"I did see her," I said. "I didn't sleep with her, and you do care."

Valerie's head was bowed. She watched her footfalls, afraid, of course, to look at me. It seemed as if her next question was stuck in her throat. Finally, she turned to me, and her hand went to the Crucifix and she twisted it maniacally.

"I'm only asking once. Do you still love her? Don't give me the bullshit answer about Anthony. Tell me straight. When you see yourself in love is it her rather than me?"

She took a step closer to me as though I wouldn't lie to her if she were closer than a foot away. I wasn't built to lie anyway.

"When I'm with her it's confusing," I said. "I know she's everything I don't want, but she has a way. Even the way she says my name is different. I don't know if that's love, but I always have to be there for her. We've been through too much."

Valerie's lower lip quivered, but she surprised me for the first time in a long while. She hugged me. This time the hug resulted in a kiss on the lips, and I brushed the hair away from her eyes with a lingering touch.

"But I know I love you too," I said. I probably would have been in better shape if I hadn't included the 'too'.

"Can't imagine the four of us living happily ever after," Valerie said. She patted her tummy. "Now tell me about the criminal adventures you've been on. Assault and murder, you've been a busy boy."

We both laughed.

I told her about the reporter and the blinding rage when he brought Anthony's name into it. I explained how Frank Powers had threatened me and that I'd left Jenna in New York.

"So who murdered him?" Valerie asked.

"I most certainly didn't, and I hope she didn't because if she did it looks an awful lot like we planned it together."

"Especially because she followed you back to Baltimore. Where's her son?"

I shrugged.

"I honestly haven't spoken to her. My cell phone is sitting back there in the car. I imagine that it's ringing off the hook."

"There isn't a hook anymore," she said. "Phones don't ring off the hook anymore. They vibrate and play music. She's going to be at your house when you get back there, you know."

"I know," I said.

"So, you still want me?" Valerie asked. "Don't feel like you have to say 'yes' either. I can handle things on my own."

She allowed me to touch her stomach. I made a grand gesture of touching her gently. "Of course I still want you," I whispered. I had no idea if I was lying or not. At that very moment, I did need her love to keep me happy, but love changes.

"No one knows you better than me," she said. "I know where you hide your secrets. I love you unconditionally. She doesn't. Just remember that."

Valerie eased away from me and turned back to the office. "I have a lot of work to do," she said. "Will you still take my Mom tomorrow?"

"Yes," I said.

"Good because she's liable to give you an earful too."

Just like that, Valerie walked away from me, twisting the Crucifix wildly as she opened the front door and disappeared in the offices of Green, Babbitt and Feinstein. Max barked her all the way in the door.

As I drove towards my home, I ignored the phone. The single thought that did not leave my mind was that I should have at least kissed Valerie. I wondered if she was thinking about the fact that we hadn't kissed as we parted. Kissing someone was such a simple gesture that meant so much. Why hadn't I kissed her?

There were two police cars in my driveway. The front door was wide open, and I caught the sight of one officer on the front walk talking to Jenna. She was drinking something out of one of my Baltimore Orioles souvenir cups.

"Perfect!" I said a bit too loudly. Max jumped in his seat and his loud barking caused every head to turn in our direction. I grabbed the cell phone from the counsel and led Max to the gated backyard. Jenna was engaged in a spirited conversation with Officer Cunningham, but she called my name as I passed. *Even the way she said my name was different.* It caused my heart to jump in my chest cavity.

A few minutes later, we gathered in the center of my living room. Jenna was dressed in a pair of tan shorts and a tight-fitting black blouse that showed every inch of her amazing body. There were three officers searching through my things, which meant there were eight eyes on her body at all times, including mine.

Jenna wasn't talking. She rested her left hand on my thigh as she rolled her eyes, sipped her drink, and every so often, wiped a tear. She wanted the officers gone so that we could be alone, but I wasn't really sure if I shared her desire. I needed my life back. Normally I would be working on a new column, watching football, and getting a good night's rest. Finally, after an exhaustive search, one of the officers (his nametag read: DiPietro) stood before me. I got to my feet and watched his eyes go to Jenna's breasts and then back to me.

"We have your answering machine message and a single black notebook," he said. He showed me the three-subject notebook that held the notes for my last seven columns.

"Why are you taking my notebook?" I asked.

"There are a lot of thoughts in here," he said. "We need to review it. We will most likely return it to you, but it has to be evaluated."

"I'm a newspaper columnist," I said. "That notebook is how I do my work. I certainly didn't confess that I wrote about murdering someone in it."

DiPietro glanced at Jenna's legs. She sighed heavily to let me know that my argument was boring her. She had been privy to my lifelong obsession of protecting my black notebook. She had once removed it from my desk to use it for a grocery list. It was the closest I had ever come to leaving her before I actually did.

"You can't take his precious notebook," Jenna said. "He'll be lost without it." She sipped from the plastic O's cup and a whiff of Crown Royal permeated the air.

"Procedure," DiPietro said. "You'll get it back."

Once more, he took in Jenna's frame.

"Are you going to stop drooling over me?" Jenna asked. "Keep your fucking eyes to yourself, please."

DiPietro's head bowed to the carpet. He tipped his hat to us and back to the door, but he couldn't help himself, he looked at Jenna one more time.

"Horney bastard," Jenna said.

I went to the side window and watched the last of the police cars back out of my driveway. I had never felt more nervous about being alone with Jenna. I made a grand gesture of staring out the front window, and all at once, I felt her hands around my waist. I turned to face her, and what might have been the worst possible thing happened.

Jenna kissed me.

CHAPTER 9

"The pleasure of love lasts but a moment.
The pain of love lasts a lifetime."
Bette Davis

We held the kiss for a full minute. Jenna's mouth was open and her tongue moved quickly, but it was senseless to think that I could stop myself from kissing her back. I tasted the crown and coke. I kissed back hungrily, all the while wondering why I hadn't kissed Valerie goodbye. When we finally separated, Jenna turned away quickly.

"Oh my God, we need to talk," she said.

Perhaps I had seen too many episodes of CSI. I held my finger to my nose to shush her. There was certainly a chance that the officers had left a recording device in the apartment. If Jenna had something to confess, I wanted her to be speaking only to me, and perhaps Max. I grabbed her hand and led her out the back door into the yard. Max came running, of course, and instead of running to me, he ran at her. He jumped up and she patted his head and sat down in one of the patio chairs. The cold wind blew, shaking the umbrella that I should have taken down and put away for the winter.

I was only going to ask the question once.

"Did you do it?"

"Of course not," Jenna said. "I loved him."

My heart jumped, and I went to her chair, kneeling on the deck before her. Max was on my right shoulder. The fact that she had not been a part of the murder would certainly make things a lot simpler. Knowing that neither of us could be implicated in the death would make the rest of it manageable.

"But I might know who did," Jenna said.

My stupid heart sank.

Sitting in the cold of the backyard wasn't doing much for either one of us.

"Let's go for a ride," I said.

Max's ears perked up as he internalized the sentence and before I could even stand up he was on me, jumping wildly.

"I guess Max is going."

The word 'going' sent Max over the edge.

"We can grab a couple of slices and talk it through."

Jenna reached for my hand, and the three of us headed for my truck.

The late evening sky was filled with low-hanging autumnal clouds. The brisk air was a memory a few minutes after I started the truck, but I had to lower the back window so that Max could watch the traffic fly by, with his face in the rush of air. Jenna started the story a few minutes after we had settled in.

"I wanted to talk to him about Tyler. Despite all that his lawyer was saying to my lawyer, I thought if I could see him or that I could change his mind. He wouldn't take my phone calls, so I drove over there. My plan was to talk to him, and then come here to be with you. I figured we could work it out later."

I drove steadily, focusing on her words and the rhythm of the cars streaming by on the four-lane of I-95.

"I knew that he'd been threatening you, and I also knew that he threatened a lot of people, including the one who I think killed him. He was trying to warn everyone around me that he would make their lives a living hell, and she didn't take it well, I imagine."

"She?" I asked. I turned my head to gauge her reaction.

"I can't tell you," Jenna said. Her voice cracked as the emotion threatened to overtake her. "Frank is a unique man," she said. "I know you wonder how it can be possible, but he makes you love him, you know? He does it with two basic principles guiding you, fear and intimidation. He is all about power. He's actually a sociopath."

I certainly didn't understand it and I wanted to say as much, but I didn't want to derail Jenna's thoughts.

"I know what you're thinking, but he's rich and he's powerful, and once you live like that, you get used to it. Anyway, Frank buys and sells affections. He controls people by being a force that can't be denied. He donates money to the big political forces. He uses hired muscle to make his point. Unfortunately, for me, and for Tyler, he needs his ego stoked at every turn. He balances it all by having the best of everything. We lived in a mansion. We ate the best food and drove the fanciest cars."

I was getting the point. I certainly couldn't see Jenna cowering to such a man, but we all get trapped to a certain extent, in a world that is different than what we had imagined.

"It *is* fun being pampered. Right or wrong, it's what I believed I *deserved* after losing Anthony."

When her voice mouthed the word 'deserved' Jenna cried. I wasn't sure how to comfort her in regard to something that was so misguided.

"It was all great as long as Frank still considered me to be the most beautiful of all the women in the world. He chased me and landed me because I fulfilled his portfolio. I was the prettiest girl in the room, and as long as that remained true, I would have a home in his mansion."

"So when did it stop being magical?" I asked.

"When I was no longer the prettiest girl in the room," Jenna said. She half-laughed and half-cried the sentence. "I knew he was screwing around and looking for a way out. Tyler was a nuisance to him, but he showed him off and talked about what a great dad he was to his son. He needed to keep up appearances, and he worked on his escape plan."

"Who did it?" I asked.

"It might be someone who loves me," Jenna said. "Or someone who saw through him. It could also be anyone else that he casted aside, or cheated somehow."

Being married to Jenna allowed me the patience. The story would come to me, but it would come out in her time.

I parked the truck in a small pizza shop, raised the back window a bit so Max couldn't escape, and met Jenna at the front door of the nearly-empty place. Jenna found a bright red booth in the far corner of the room, and I grabbed three slices of pizza and two bottles of root beer at the front counter. She was staring off into space by the time I placed the food in front of her.

"The list of suspects will be long," she whispered.

There was one other couple in the room, but the two young people were scarfing down their slices and staring down at their cell phones. I'm not even sure they knew we were there.

"As long as we clear our names we don't have to worry about it." Jenna raised the pizza to her mouth. A string of cheese made it clear back to the paper plate in front of her. She chewed quickly.

"The police know you didn't do it because you were here. They know I didn't do it because I didn't pull up to the gate until they'd already discovered him. They know I didn't shoot a gun, and they also know that I have a receipt, with the time on it, for a pair of shoes I purchased ten minutes before they figure he was killed."

"So you're in the clear," I said. "You know who did it?"

"Not by name," Jenna said. She sipped the root beer and her eyes threatened tears. "I saw someone speeding away from the scene," Jenna said.

I set the half-eaten slice on the plate.

"Did you see the killer?" I asked.

"Certainly." Jenna said. "One of his sluts. I'll never testify against her.

As we ate our slices and sipped the soda, we talked about the immediate future. Her presence in my life was problematic to me, but Jenna didn't seem to consider it.

"What am I going to do?" Jenna asked. "What is Tyler doing right now? Does he know? Does my boy miss me? The lawyers have him in seclusion. I don't want to go home. Do you mind? Can I stay with you?"

I had not even mentioned Valerie and the new child growing inside of her. She couldn't possibly know because in all of the years of being with Jenna it had never really been about me. We lived our life trapped in Jenna's world. It was the way it would always be.

"Of course you can stay," I said.

I gathered the crust from the pizza. When we got back into the truck, I handed them over to Max. Valerie hated when I fed Max as if he were a human. Jenna thought it was the greatest thing in the world.

"We should have got him a slice," she said.

"He likes the meat lover's special," I answered.

As I drove back to the apartment, my cell phone sounded. Out of habit, I answered it. My editor's voice met my ear.

"You're there," he said. "They want your column back. Your criminal acts are receiving so much play that they want to sell more papers. Your assignment tonight is to get me a new column. Can you do one called 'Everything I Know About Chaos?' You and I know it will be complete, worthless psychobabble bullshit, but the readers are a bunch of fucking morons."

I laughed. I glanced over at Jenna who was trying to get Max to sit in her lap. Her smile was simply a light for the inside of that truck. She was the very definition of chaos.

"I can pull it off," I said.

"Good, e-mail it to me by morning."

I set the phone in the counsel.

"Good news?" Jenna asked.

"I got my job back," I said. "They want me to write a column about chaos."

Jenna gave up her attempt to let Max sit on her lap. Instead, she eased closer to me and grabbed my right hand. I drove the rest of the way back to the apartment holding her hand in mine. How's that for chaos?

**

Once we returned to my apartment, the plan was for me to shower while Jenna relaxed in bed with the television and Max for company. She found a rerun of the **King of Queens**, and she stretched out on my bed and Max rested his big head on her chest.

"Hurry back," she called. "We need to get some wine in this house tomorrow."

The last thing I wanted to do was get her a supply of wine, but something told me I'd be at a liquor store before tomorrow ended.

The warm shower was just what my tired bones needed. The idea for the column on handling chaos was coming to me in bits and pieces as I washed my hair. Writing had always been easy for me. One thought after the next, all psychobabble bullshit, for sure, but if it meant something to someone, it was worth it. It was all just one word after another. Why didn't everyone write to sort out their thoughts?

I toweled off in front of the steamed mirror, almost hoping that Jenna would be asleep when I returned to the room. I had no idea how I could resist slipping in beside her, but I had to, for Valerie, for my new child. It dawned on me that I should be excited, but when I thought of Valerie's pregnancy all that came to mind was chaos.

Back in the room, Jenna was wide-awake. She was also naked. Max was on the floor, and Jenna stretched out on the bed with the remote in her hand.

"I forgot what it's like to be poor," she said.

"What happened to your clothes?" I asked. Of course, it was

impossible to not look.

"Come on, Sal, you know better than that. I didn't do it to scare you, I like to be naked. You used to like me naked too."

I diverted my eyes. She was something else. Her entire world had crumbled. She had no idea where her son was for the night. Her husband was dead, and she was comfortable enough in her own skin to let me see every inch of her.

"Tell me about your girlfriend," she said.

I turned away. I was caught thinking about how I was going to drop my towel and change in my own room, and she had floored me with the question.

"I don't really have a girlfriend," I said.

I had denied Valerie again.

"Well, your girlfriend's mommy called when you were in the shower. She wanted to make sure you were going to pick her up for her chemo."

I pulled my underwear on before dropping the towel. If felt as if my entire life up to that moment had been cancelled and that everything I knew was null and void and chaotic.

"I'm going with you," she said. "Elaine invited me."

Jenna scooted forward on the bed. Max sensed the movement and he jumped up to join her. "Would you feel more comfortable if I dressed?" she asked.

"Yes, it would make it easier to tell you about Valerie."

Jenna got off the bed. She reached me in a split-second and her arms were around my neck even quicker than that.

"I won't fuck up your life," she whispered. "But don't cut me out."

"I couldn't if I wanted to," I whispered back.

Our bare chests were touching. How could I simply deny *our* love? When it is all broken down, love rarely shows itself in such raw terms. Who is dumb enough to deny it when it is right there to be held? Jenna hugged me tightly and then just as quickly broke away. What she had said finally made its way to my brain.

"What do you mean you're going with us tomorrow?"

"Elaine invited me for a ham and cheese melt at Denny's. She said she wants to meet me."

Twenty minutes later, I had my laptop on my lap. Jenna and Max were sharing my bed, and I was in the dark living room, tapping on the keys until I finished my thoughts about chaos. I needed to figure out how I would make it through the next day, the next week, and the rest of my days on the planet.

Everything I Know About Living in Chaos

Do you know people who thrive on chaos every single day of their lives? You must know what I am talking about here. There are people who enjoy the drama of having one personal emergency after another. It almost seems to me that some people aren't happy unless they are absolutely miserable. It also dawns on me that there is a real simple solution.

When we are in control of our emotions, we have power. When our emotions control us, the results are very often treacherous. Many of the troubles in life comes from the fact that there are so many of us that can't be still. We are looking for instant stimulation in a world where every single thing is at our fingertips, but chasing peace in a torrent of a cyclone is difficult at best, and impossible at worst.

It is important to remember that the cyclone derives its power from a calm center, and so does man. As Ralph Waldo Emerson, a calm man, was known to say, 'Nothing can bring you peace but yourself.'

The real power to meet life head-on is developed, in the deep centers of quietness, where the soul and the mind meet God. Man should not try to think without a peaceful mind. Some of the great deep thinkers remind us to use aggressive activation when assessing a chaotic situation. Simply put, instead of responding emotionally, practice doing something constructive about the situation. Store up moments of happiness as a squirrel hoards chestnuts. You must use those moments of happiness in the middle of the chaotic mess that has taken control of your heart and mind.

How is it done, you ask?

First off, don't race your motor. Moderation in all is the key. We've all heard it a million times. We've all said it a half-a-million times. It's true. Work, play and eat at a leisurely pace. Don't let your mind and body wear down. Forgive grievances. Stay calm and serene in the face of the rising waters. It isn't easy to do, but do your best and surrender the rest. Try not to be apprehensive with what tomorrow will bring. Put your trust in your own abilities to see things clearly. Forget fear and trust God or a higher power. You will see that doing such things will allow you to understand everything you know about ridding your life of chaos."

Amen award for this guy!

CHAPTER 10

"The gods conceal from men the happiness of death,
that they may endure life."
Lucan

As I showered on Monday morning, a palpable sense of dread threatened to overtake me. I considered the dynamic of Elaine and Jenna, and how the situation, with two strong-willed women could go immediately south. Yet as I dressed for the day ahead, I used a bit of my own mind cleansing to get through. Reacting to situations in life was the real key. I had an open mind about it. Before entering the shower, I called Elaine and spoke briefly with her, asking her to take it easy on Jenna. Given the personalities of the two women, I had no idea how it might play out.

Jenna and Max were waiting on the back porch. Jenna had both hands wrapped around a mug of coffee, and Max was at her feet. The sun was climbing in the early morning sky, and although it was brisk, Jenna looked extremely comfortable wrapped in a tan blanket that covered her shoulders.

"Good morning," she said as I pushed the sliding glass door open. She moved her legs so that I could squeeze in beside her. Max jumped to greet me, but quickly settled back into position as I sat. The newspaper was open on the table beside Jenna. It was folded so that she could read my column about chaos, which evidently hadn't needed much editing.

"Am I one of those dramatic people?" she asked.

I laughed, and she quickly joined in.

"You think?"

The coffee was strong and hot. I took a small sip, and even breathed it in.

"I spoke to my lawyer this morning. They want to talk with me again. They asked me a couple of questions about some of his other women. The cops obviously found something. I can't believe that this is actually my life. The assault charges against you are, most likely going to be dropped today. My agent has been receiving some interesting offers about my next acting job. I even spoke with Tyler. He's off to school already."

She announced it all as though she was giving me the bus route, but she flicked a tear away from her right eye as she finished up.

"It should be easier than this," she said.

A cool breeze swept across the porch and Max shifted, thought about getting up, and then just lowered his head again.

"I think about God now and again," Jenna said. "I'm not a big fan."

Elaine would be waiting patiently for us. I wanted to let Jenna know that there wasn't a lot of leeway when it came to leaving Elaine waiting, but Jenna was not contemplative very often. I decided to go for it.

"A lot on your mind this morning, huh?"

"Every morning I open my eyes and think of Anthony," she said. "I try to picture him in my mind. Would he look more like you or me? Would he be happy? What would his laugh sound like? I think of Frank and Tyler and how I tried to compensate for the pain. I was going to be a star, and that would make up for everything. It would fill the hole of losing Anthony."

"But it didn't?"

"No, and being a celebrity didn't help either. It's all a bunch of shit, you know? The real important things can't be bought or sold. I'm going to miss Frank too. I know you can't understand it, but it's true."

The fact that she was trying to put it all together was strange. Perhaps, she seemed to understand that most of what is supposed to be important is fleeting.

"You're in for a treat today," I said. "Elaine is going to make sure you realize a whole lot more about life than you did before you set eyes on her."

A half an hour later we were on our way to pick up Elaine for her treatment. The trip to Elaine's home was dominated by silence. The usually rambunctious Jenna was content to sit quietly, rubbing Max's ears as he nudged his big head in the space between the two of us. If my decision of women were left to Max it would be a complete mismatch.

Elaine emerged from the front door as we entered the driveway.

"I'll go help her," Jenna said.

"Don't you dare," I started to say, but Jenna was already out the door.

"Leave me the hell alone," I heard Elaine say as Jenna arrived by her side.

Oh yeah, this was going to be beautiful.

Jenna ran back to the car as if she had been slapped. She sat down, turned to me and started to laugh.

"Holy shit! She doesn't like to be helped."

"Get in the back," I yelled. "She isn't going to sit in the back."

Jenna hustled out of the car and into the backseat as Elaine struggled to get into the seat that beside me.

"We're off to a rousing start," Elaine said.

Her face looked a bit more drawn to me and the bags under her eyes were heavy.

"Good morning, dumbass," she said to me. "With all that you've been up to, I must admit that I would've lost a bet about you showing up today."

I leaned in and kissed Elaine on the left cheek. She hardly noticed. Instead, she turned to Jenna.

"Sorry if I was rude in the driveway," she said, "but I hate when people treat me like an old lady. I'm sorry about the murder too."

There it was, pure Elaine. She would put it all out there for consideration, immediately. Jenna extended her hand and Elaine let it just hang there over the top of the seat.

"I don't shake hands, dear," she said. "I made it a rule when it occurred to me that people dig shit out of their noses, ears and asses. Nothing personal, but I don't want to touch your hand."

So, with pleasantries having been exchanged, I pulled out into traffic as Elaine and Jenna headed down the road of getting to know one another.

"I used to watch you on that soap opera," Elaine said. "I didn't

CLIFFORD JAMES FAZZOLARI

care for you much."

"I was playing a villain," Jenna said. "I'm glad you didn't like me. It means I'm a good actress."

Elaine seemed to consider that for a moment and just before answering, she winked at me.

"I don't think that's it," she said. "I just didn't care for you."

Jenna screamed in horror.

"Don't get me wrong, you're beautiful, but you struck me as a spoiled bitch. You aren't a spoiled bitch, are you?"

This time, Jenna laughed. She was getting both barrels of the Elaine gun.

"Would Sal have married me if I'd been a spoiled bitch?" Jenna asked.

Again, Elaine took a moment before responding.

"Probably," she said. "He's a dumbass, and he's led astray by beauty. That's why he loves me."

Traffic was moving slowly as we were smack dab in the middle of morning rush hour. Usually Elaine and I were in full discussion of my morning column and before I even thought about missing it, she brought up my idea of chaos.

"I liked the column this morning. Everyone is always so busy and so dramatic. People don't realize that they are going to die someday and that all of this running around will have been for nothing."

The only difference in our discussion was that today, Jenna had the first opinion.

"Do you think about death a lot?" she asked Elaine.

"More as I start knocking on its door," Elaine said, "but if I were in awe of death I'd be cheating myself out of life, don't you think?

The train is coming sooner or later I won't have a choice but to get on board. Death is a great hiding spot for tired old ladies."

In all the years that we'd been together and even after Anthony died Jenna had avoided the topic of death. Given the fact that Frank had just died her interest seemed to be piqued. Elaine had that sort of effect on people.

"So you aren't scared?"

"I'm not looking forward to it," Elaine said. "What the hell am I going to do? They say that death begins with life's first breath and that life begins with the touch of death."

Elaine waited for that to sink in. She smiled.

"A lot of shit by people who have no other choice but to accept that we are all going to die."

"I run from grief," she said. Her voice was softer now. "I'm so sad today. I've been so lonely for so long. I haven't been doing anything but hiding for years."

By the time, Jenna completed the sentence she was crying.

"That is too bad," Elaine whispered. "I really feel for you losing your son, but if your husband was murdered there's something more than meets the eye. But, look at you, you're a beautiful young woman. Life certainly would've been easier for me if I looked like that. You can't cheat your life by worrying about death."

Jenna fought hard to keep the tears at bay. For the first time in her life, she was actually listening. I wasn't sure what to do with the new Jenna.

"Put it this way," Elaine said. "Life is a gift from God, or so we're told. If God wants his gift back at some point, who are we to bitch about it?"

Jenna couldn't accept that so casually, especially not in light of Anthony's short life.

"He took my baby away before Anthony had the chance to live!"

"He did Anthony a favor," Elaine said. "He died before he did something that cost him his soul. We all have a chance to throw our soul into the abyss. God knows there's plenty out there that can go wrong. We can become great actresses that everyone fawns over until we think our shit doesn't stink and we smash everything that's special into little pieces."

Elaine was blessed with a great gift. She delivered a great insult that made Jenna laugh. She had been doing the same thing to me since the day I met her.

The slow-moving miles were controlled by an awkward silence.

"Let me ask you this," Jenna said. "You've lost people in your life. How do you deal with the pain?"

I negotiated a move to the right lane so that we could make the exit.

"There's no dealing with it," Elaine said. "Don't take it personally, but you aren't smart enough to figure it all out. None of us are, honey. It's you that you have to work on. The great train is coming for you too."

I'd heard Elaine's words before, but they were profound and searing to me as I watched them bite into Jenna.

"Dumb-dumb here is on-board," Elaine said. "He writes beautiful words every day. He's off-the-beam a little now, and putting my daughter through hell, but he'll figure it out. He knows that before you run, you have to learn how to fall."

I pulled into the parking lot at the doctor's office. Elaine turned to me. Jenna was silent. That, in and of itself, was a minor miracle. I turned to Elaine.

"Time to fry those titties," I said, and we both laughed.

This time, Jenna knew enough not to help Elaine handle the walk from the car to the door.

"She really is something," Jenna whispered.

I took my ex-wife's hand as we made our way across the lot. It was a long-forgotten gesture and one that wasn't lost on Elaine.

"How nice," she said. "Do you like ham and cheese melts?" Elaine asked Jenna.

"No way!" Jenna said. "It would take me three weeks to work off the fat!"

"Tough shit," Elaine said. "You're having one."

An hour later, we were seated at Denny's. This time, we weren't alone. A news reporter had followed us in and set up camp at the table across the way. The scandal was fresh. The tall, young man who wore gold-rimmed glasses was looking for a quote from Jenna.

"You need a quote?" Elaine asked as we settled into the booth.

The man nodded, took out portable recorder and smiled. Jenna's beautiful face was home to an ear-to-ear grin.

"Don't sweat the petty things and don't pet the sweaty things," Elaine said. "Now get the hell out of here before we call the cops. I get one good meal a week. Spoil it and I'll rip your nuts off."

The man shuffled away as our booth and the two booths surrounding us erupted in laughter.

"That's a George Carlin line," Elaine explained. "That man was a genius."

We ate our sandwiches, talking lightly about the universe and our particular places in it.

"I've never had a better morning than that," Jenna said as we dropped Elaine back home.

"Don't mess up dumbass," Elaine said. "He needs to take care of my daughter."

Before leaving the truck, Elaine turned to me. I had taken very little heat all morning.

"I have your next column for you. Tell them everything you know about making decisions," she said. "A successful life hinges on making a higher percentage of wise choices versus stupid mistakes."

"I'll get started on it," I said. Elaine, with her choice of column topics, had very subtly explained what she expected of me.

"It was a pleasure to meet you," she said to Jenna. "I like you a lot more than the characters you play. You're a beautiful woman on the outside. Bring that beauty in."

With that, Elaine was out of the vehicle. I lowered the side window.

"I'll pick you up on Wednesday," I called. "I love you!"

Elaine answered without turning around. She flipped me the bird.

Everything I Know About Making the Right Decisions

A successful life hinges on making a higher percentage of wise choices versus stupid mistakes. It is easy to make a mistake. A lapse in judgment is possible in every waking moment. We make mistakes because of inner conflict, because of resentment, out of feelings of guilt and frustration. Sometimes they are mistakes that do not allow us room to recover. The greatest mistake that we can make is to let an error in judgment strip us of faith in ourselves.

There is a right and a wrong way to live life. I believe that living right is based on a number of true scientific principles. If you break the laws of science, your life may go terribly wrong. Common sense will tell you that making honest, unselfish and right decisions will allow you to lead a more peaceful life.

Unfortunately, we can't see very far down the road. In a lot of instances this shortsightedness costs us in the end. Realizing this should provide enough instruction to make each step true. Put each foot down in wisdom and faith, and turn your stumbling blocks into stepping stones.

Sometimes the decisions that we need to make don't come easily. We are driven face first into the ground ahead as we trip on the past mistakes that we don't disregard as useless baggage. In some instances, it is fear of moving forward that stops us in our tracks. By keeping your energy levels high, and believing in your solid heart, you will discourage those fears.

Ask yourself 'Am I doing the right thing?'

Ask that question over in your mind and before long, you'll know everything I know about making the right decisions.

CHAPTER 11

"Give expression to the noble desires
that lie in your heart."
Gordon B. Hinckley

My eyes opened slowly and I closed them again, realizing that it was the next morning and that I'd had more than a few glasses of wine the night before. Jenna had talked deep into the night and it was too early to be awake, but when I rubbed my hands across my eyes I knew that sleep for the night was over. It was time to rise and face the music.

My open eyes settled in on the fact that I was on the couch, fully dressed, and alone. Max, who usually slept in close proximity, was nowhere to be found. I plucked my watch from the end table: 7:23. At least I'd slept for a few hours. I lifted my head slowly and saw the empty wine bottles on the kitchen table. I remembered opening the second one. Who had opened the third?

My mouth was dry and I brought my hands to my lips and remembered kissing Jenna so deeply. I knew that it had ended right after the long kiss. She had escaped to the back bedroom, and after giving a half-hearted effort to be invited in, I had settled on the couch. Even the dog left me to my own devices.

As I got used to the rhythmic pounding of my head and the pain behind my eyes I appreciated that Jenna had shown restraint. Her little afternoon out with Elaine had a profound effect on her, but where would it lead us now?

I thought of all of my old problem-solving techniques. What did I want out of the situation? A lot of people live blindly, reacting to one thing after another, never figuring out exactly what was best for them. It was something that I really needed to do. If I could have all my wishes granted, what would they be? I needed to figure that out first. Being up early, would allow me the time to sort it through, but I had to pee first.

Finishing my bathroom visit, I entered the kitchen and hit the button to start the coffeemaker. When I shuffled past the kitchen table, I saw the note stuck between the salt and pepper shakers.

"Me and Max are out for a run! I'll take care of him! I love him more than I love you!"

My love for her had grown. There was no doubt about that, but where did it leave us? What three wishes, if granted, would make my life complete? Would I choose my ex-wife and my dead child, or my future wife and my unborn child? Was it up to me to choose?

I filled a tall Baltimore Orioles commemorative glass with water from the tap and I chugged it down in one gulp.

Jenna had confessed that she most likely didn't really love Frank. "It was all about being a star," she had said. "We all want to be big stars. We all crave attention. We talk about wanting to live a nice, peaceful life, but we want to be noticed."

The ham and cheese melt with Elaine had done wonders

for Jenna. The more wine we drank the night before, the more I knew that it would be different from here on out.

"Elaine is the star of her life!" Jenna had exclaimed. "She isn't afraid of intimacy, or loneliness. She laughs when she wants, and she cries when it matters. I want to be like her. I want to love with everything I have and leave it all on the table!"

We had toasted Elaine.

My head was throbbing. I filled the O's glass again. How could we all live together? Was it possible to love two women? Was there a chance to share my life with Jenna, Elaine and Valerie? Could I father a child with my heart in turmoil and my head in shambles?

The thought of my next column crept into the back corner of my mind. I poured a mug of coffee, and headed to the couch, balancing the coffee, my new black notebook and a thin black pen. How much longer could I write a column about knowing shit when I had no idea what I really understood about being alive?

Mindlessly I punched up my editor on my contacts list and John answered on the third ring. As usual, I had caught him in the middle of chewing something. Our relationship had become solid through the years, but I couldn't resist the urge to tease him.

"Whopper or Big Mac?" I asked.

"Very funny," he said. "It's a fucking rice cake. My wife is making me eat these things because evidently I'm fucking fat."

Despite my wine-induced headache I laughed.

"Seriously, did you ever eat one of these things? I'd rather wash my big, fat ass with it. By the way, has it ever dawned on you to swing by the office? I know we are still paying you, right?"

"You got my column," I said.

"We've been over this," John said. "I get my ass chewed every time she thinks you're mailing the columns in. You have to at least show your ugly face."

"I know. I'll be by. I've been arrested for assault, questioned for murder and I'm with my ex-wife as my pregnant girlfriend stews in the background."

John laughed boisterously. "I'd take all of that on if I could have a fucking pizza sub."

"I'll be by today sometime," I said as my call waiting beeped. "I'll bring you a sandwich."

"That's terrific! What's the column about today?"

"Everything I know about joy," I said. "Call it 'Joy to Your World'".

Once more John's laugh was uproarious. "I knew this whole thing was shit," he said. "He's got one foot in jail and his girl is going to yank off his pecker and he's writing about joy."

There was a beep on the line and I clicked the phone over without even answering John. He definitely had a point.

"This is Cunningham," the cop said when I brought his end of the telephone to life.

"Leo here," I answered trying to sound light and breezy.

"Good morning," Cunningham said. "We'd like to know if you and your ex-wife can swing by today so perhaps we can clear you in the case?"

I went for the water glass again, but lifting it let me know that it was empty. I headed to the sink as the question sunk into my weary brain.

"We haven't been cleared?"

"Probably the wrong way to put it," Cunningham said. "We have a suspect in custody. We'd like to go over a couple of things with both of you."

The water took its time in getting cold, but before long, I had refilled the glass. I took a quick slug before answering. My curiosity was definitely piqued.

"Who is it?" I asked.

"We'd rather speak with the two of you," Cunningham said.

"Give us a couple of hours," I said.

"The sooner the better," Cunningham answered. "The media is swarming the station and most likely your front yard."

I covered the ground between the kitchen and the living room quickly. I hadn't even considered that the press might be camped out in my driveway. Evidently, Cunningham had made his point because the line went dead in my ear.

The column ideas were already popping into my head, but the mixed messages swirling in my mind had more to do with Jenna than they did with joy. I thought of Socrates saying that the hottest love has the coldest end. I wasn't sure why such a thing would jump to the front of my mind at precisely that moment, but it was the way the writing game worked. I didn't want to put too much stock into such a thought.

I moved the shade to glance out the front window being sure not to make a spectacle of myself. There were three television vans parked directly across the street. How did Jenna live in such a manner? She said that she wanted attention, but how could she possibly keep everything straight? Didn't all the cameras give her false illusions? How did she handle it day in and day out?

I was just about to let the shade snap back into position when

I saw Jenna and Max make their approach. Jenna was in a bright red jogging suit. Her long blonde hair bounced as she ran right by the camera vans. Max was in stride and neither of them seemed to notice the three reporters who exited the vans and ran in step behind them. Finally, Max turned and barked and two of the three reporters slowed considerably. Jenna just kept right on running, straight towards the front door. Not much had changed. She was still beautiful enough to make me stop and stare. I scrambled to open the front door as she turned on the walk. Max was thrilled to see me and he actually passed Jenna and made it through the door first. The reporters seemed to tire of the chase, but there were certainly camera flashes. I closed the door on them as we headed to the couch. Jenna took the water glass from my hand, and leaned in to kiss my cheek.

"He opens the door with a glass of water for me as I finish my run. You see why I love you?"

Max went immediately to his water bowl as well and he slobbered water all over the kitchen floor as he refreshed himself.

"How far did you go?" I asked.

"Four miles," Jenna said. She drained the glass and handed it to me. "A little more, please?"

For the fourth time that morning I filled the water glass as Jenna flopped down on the couch and Max jumped up in the seat next to her.

"You know what I thought of when I was running?" Jenna asked.

"What's that?" I asked casually.

"It's going to sound funny coming from me, but Elaine has had an influence."

I handed her the water, and she leaned forward and smiled. She patted the arm of the couch and I sat beside her, looking straight down into her beautiful television-star eyes.

"As I ran it occurred to me that you can run away from anything in this life but a wounded soul. You just can't go fast enough to get away from that."

"You thought of that?" I asked.

Jenna looked a little uncomfortable. She flashed a smile, but quickly bowed her head. "Wouldn't it be nice if I hadn't treated you as a house guest? I should have been there for you as you grieved Anthony. We could have made it through the storm."

I slipped my arm around her right shoulder and she leaned into me. I was also fighting back tears that I wasn't sure were still inside. I hadn't cried for what we'd lost for a long time, but it was on my shoulders through all that time.

"There's no easy way to live broken-hearted," I said. "And I don't think that the wound of the soul actually heals. We carry it through to the end. It ages us. It pains us. There has yet to be an operation for its repair."

Jenna felt so comfortable in my arms. She turned her face up to meet mine, and there was a long moment to consider which road we would take to try to repair the long-standing, gaping wound.

"I love you with everything I have," she said. "I think of your future wife and child, and I know that I shouldn't feel bad for my love, because you will take it with you into your new life."

The desire to kiss her was too much to handle. Yet as I leaned in to do just that something wonderfully strange happened. Jenna jumped up off the couch and did a full pirouette in front of me.

"Not going to happen!" she said. "We're having dinner with Elaine and Valerie tonight. This is off-limits to you." She waved her hands down her body. "I'm going to fix that wounded soul," she said as she pointed to the center of my chest.

"Dinner with Valerie and Elaine?" I asked. Max jumped off the couch at the sound of my voice and he headed straight for Jenna's legs.

"Yep, I talked to Elaine as I was running. I spoke to my lawyer too." She looked to Max and patted the top of his head. Max licked her hand. "I know who killed Frank."

"Kayla?"

"No," Jenna said. "I actually feel bad that I thought she did. It was actually one of his side-sluts, Rebecca. I don't even know who she is. Turns out, she's the jealous sort. She gave a full confession. She said the dirty bastard deserved it and that she should get a medal for ridding the world of his cheating ass."

Jenna didn't get the entire sentence out before breaking down. She flopped on the couch beside me. I stroked her golden hair as Max jumped to the couch and rested his wet nose on my left arm. As Jenna cried, I considered that I had a hard deadline to write a column about joy.

Everything I Know About Joy

As you give joy, you will receive joy. It seems like a wonderfully simple concept, doesn't it? Yet joy does in fact grow as you give it away, just as surely as it diminishes if you try to keep it to yourself.

Unless you give it, you will lose it.

It is not easy to hang onto joy in your heart. Sometimes it certainly pays to list some of the joyful moments of your life as fact. Living with joy in your world can be accomplished through practice.

Don't believe me?

Try a little experiment.

Begin your day with a joyful thought. Tell yourself that you are glad to be alive. Stand tall. Think tall. Believe tall. Joy will follow if you learn how to be happy. Quit hating people. Stop holding grudges. Don't just think about yourself.

Give your joy away.

Do you know people who always seem to be 'up?' They have learned the secret, understanding that negative and dark thoughts freeze personality. They understand that there are no true earthly riches, and that folks aren't truly rich unless they find their riches inside, and then, and this is the important part:

Share their abundance of riches.

That is Everything I Know About Joy.

CHAPTER 12

"The wise man in the storm prays to God, not for safety from danger, but for deliverance from fear."
Ralph Waldo Emerson

The wait for a table was an hour and a half at the Outback Steakhouse. The place was also so crowded that I dropped the women off at the front door and was stuck parking the car six blocks away on a residential street. By the time I walked back to the restaurant Valerie had signed us up for a table. She was holding tightly to the buzzer they gave her to alert us when the table was ready. Jenna sat on the bench holding the right hand of her new best friend, Elaine, while I stood above Valerie, rubbing her shoulders and thinking of what to think about my new crazy world. All around us the work staff buzzed from door to table, ushering in other patrons. Elaine and Jenna were engrossed in a conversation that was just out of earshot.

"We could go somewhere else," I said.

"Tell that to blooming onion, over there," Valerie said. "She's been talking about it since Jenna brought it up."

It was so hard to imagine what was going on in Valerie's mind. We hadn't even bothered to speak about much of anything, but she was here with us so that said something.

"Pretty strange situation, huh?" I finally said.

"Mom said something to me that made a lot of sense."

"Go figure," I said.

"She said, 'You can't start something completely new until all old debts are paid.' She assures me that you love me, and she better be right or I'll kill both of you."

I laughed.

"And despite the fact that I want to hate your ex-wife, I don't. Now that there's a child with me I can't imagine how she felt when Anthony died. You've never found your way around it, either, so maybe we can do it together. If I leave her with Mom long enough we're liable to figure it all out."

I took a drink order and headed off to the bar to pass the time as we waited. The bartender was a young woman with soft brown eyes that reflected the pace of her job. She smiled in my direction and I ordered four diet Cokes. Jenna had agreed not to drink alcohol, which was the first of many miracles of the evening. I handed off two of the drinks and headed back for the second set, and Valerie joined Elaine and Jenna's conversation. I watched as Elaine said something that sent both women into fits of laughter. Jenna's presence was attracting a bit of attention, but she was as low profile as I had ever seen her.

The young bartender smiled as she handed back my change. She made a half-turn away from me before whipping her head back in my direction.

"Aren't you the newspaper guy?" she asked.

I nodded.

"How's your wife?" she asked. "Oh, I just love your life! I read every word you write."

"Thank you," I said. "I'm not sure that my life is something to love right now. My ex-wife is over there talking to my girlfriend and my girlfriend's mother."

One of the other patrons called for the bartender's attention, but she was around the end of the bar positioning herself for a glimpse of Jenna. Her fascination with my life was unsettling, and the man waiting for his beer was growing more impatient.

"Listen," I said. "We'll stop by and see you after we eat," I promise.

"Oh, please do!" The girl shrieked. "You've taught me through the years that we're all connected. I feel like I know you!"

I extended my hand and she shook it with both of hers.

"Don't ever stop writing," she said, and she moved to her beer-swilling customer. "Don't forget to stop by!"

As I headed back to the bench, I thought about what she had said. 'We are all connected.'

"The buzzer is going off!" Jenna yelled to me and every single head turned in her direction.

I thought of all the people who envied her, and to a lesser extent those who believed that I had it all figured out. Valerie had said that perhaps there would be a moment where we would be able to figure it all out.

"Nobody every figures it out," I whispered to myself as I shrugged by a middle-aged couple who was shuffling to replace us on the little bench. *But, maybe we ARE all connected.*

I wrote the next day's column, in my mind, as we shared our meal.

***

Everything I Know about Being Connected

We have meteors crashing into Russia and asteroids screaming by the Earth close enough to see.

Strange, right?

It blows my mind when I think about the fact that the asteroid is the size of a couple of football fields and it's gliding on by. When you think about all that has gone on while the universe is spinning, you get that we are but a speck of that time.

Think of that when you are waiting in line behind the guy as he clicks through his lottery picks.
Time passes slowly there, right?

We argue over the most mundane and senseless stuff. We entertain ourselves by watching bad behavior. We are trying desperately to amuse ourselves to death, but consider this much when you are thinking about your days.

The other night I woke from a dream thinking: 'We're all connected.'

I had no idea what it could mean.

Are we all connected?

I am not just talking about me and you here. I am actually considering everyone all through time.

I have become fond of saying that love kicks death's ass and that no one who is truly loved ever dies, but it might be more than that. I consider that those who have gone before us are still alive in so many ways. Their spirit, their lives, their heartbeat is still part of the fabric of everything that has ever happened.

Too deep?

Think of it this way.

Those people aren't gone because things they said and did still enter your mind in all kinds of ways, like when something similar happens, or in dreams, or in the eyes of the children they left behind, or in the way they lit up your heart.

It is not as if they are gone, but that they are actually in another city or state, just out of physical reach.

They surely aren't out of mental reach, right?

They certainly still have a spiritual presence.

They are in your laugh.

They are in your tears.

They just are.

Another thing to consider:

Imagine the first time that you went on a date. Can you remember that? It is sort of a common experience, right?

Do you remember the butterflies in your stomach the first time you reached to hold her hand, or the first time that he reached for your hand?

Do you recall the movie you saw or the dance that you attended?

Can't you almost imagine all of it once more?

It is not gone!

The moment has passed but it is still really alive.

Don't believe me?

I was in 8th grade and the dance was held in the dimly lit high school gym. The class banner was strung on the back wall and I remember thinking that graduation day was so far away.

There was a knot in my stomach because I couldn't dance. My mouth was dry because I was nervous when it came to talking to a girl.

Yet somehow, there I was with a pretty girl as a date. She was in an off-white dress. She wore glasses, but she was pretty enough to pull it off.

My tie felt like it was choking me. She was concerned that her friends were being rude. I heard my Mom's voice in my head, 'Be a gentleman.'

I got my date a plastic cup filled with really red punch, and she smiled when she thanked me.

Time went quickly that night but here it is, alive, almost 40 years later.

Every moment.

Before long, we were alone. We walked towards the local restaurant to meet up with our friends. I was thinking about getting a great burger and a plate of curly fries. I can still almost taste those curly fries covered in ketchup and vinegar.

Halfway across the lawn at the front of the high school I finally reached for her hand.

I recall all the minutes that passed, so slowly, as I worked up the courage to do it.

As I wrote that sentence just now, I felt the nervousness creep up inside of me again.
The butterflies are still alive.

She slid her hand into mine, and I felt the stickiness of the sweaty coupling. Was her hand sweating or was it mine? What did she think?

That moment is not gone.

It is out there in the air, alive between two people who have not physically seen one another in about thirty years.

But it's alive.

And that's where the connections go, on and on, all of us together.

The shared experiences of being connected somewhere.

The love stays.

The hate stays.

The laughter stays.

The tears stay.

Happiness and sadness are co-mingled in our community of being.

Our bodies go.

Our spirit doesn't.

Maybe one day that asteroid will strike the Earth, but the universe will just keep right on spinning, and all that we did here will continue.

Through eternity.

***

As we headed out of the restaurant, the crowd began to form around Jenna. A young girl with a steel rod through her nostrils was the first in line to request an autograph and a photo, and I watched as Jenna went into full superstar mode. She wrapped an arm around the girl's bare shoulder and flashed that million-dollar smile.

"Why don't you get the car while Marilyn Monroe mugs for these people?" Elaine asked.

I glanced quickly at Valerie who returned a quick smile before turning her attention back to Jenna's movie star moves. I had seen every single move before. For one reason or another, I was having a hard time looking away – from Valerie. I kissed Valerie on the left cheek and started to turn away.

"What am I chopped liver?" Elaine asked. She turned in her seat on the bench in front of the restaurant. She was also pointing at her cheek. I leaned in and kissed her quickly.

"These people are like sheep," she said. "Why do they get all googly-eyed for someone just because they're on television?"

"Their own lives are boring," I said. "But I'm not bored, I'm blessed."

"You *are* blessed," Elaine said. "You're with three hot broads. You should never forget how lucky you are."

The crowd was picking up more people as I turned to walk away. I heard men and women of all ages screaming about how amazing it was that Jenna was standing right there. I zipped my light coat up tight for the six-block walk. The evening air was still and the street lights illuminated a mostly barren sidewalk. There were still people walking quickly down the sidewalk for their chance to glimpse Jenna and I smiled as I watched my own footfalls.

I made the right turn down the residential street and walked along in the gathering dark to the car that was halfway down the block. I heard the first of a series of pops that sounded like a backfiring car, but the sounds didn't truly register. I just kept thinking of what Elaine had said. I truly was a blessed man, and somehow we would work it all out. Jenna would figure out her life without Frank, and Valerie, Elaine and the baby would give me the life I finally wanted. Life had turned me upside down, shook me hard, and landed me back on my feet, ready for the full charge ahead. This was the first night of the rest of my life, as the story goes.

I started the car and immediately heard five more loud pops.

"What the hell is that?"

I turned the car off and listened, and all at once, it registered.

Someone was shooting a gun. I started the car again and slammed it into drive. Was someone shooting up the sidewalk?

I lowered the driver's side window as I turned the car and quickly covered the road to the front door of the restaurant. The crowd was scattering and people were running wildly through the street. The pop-pop-pop just kept going and with each shot the bedlam grew. In the middle of the bedlam, I spotted him. He was dressed in full military regalia with a helmet and fatigues. He was holding a long rifle in his hand and from a crouched position he was simply moving in a circle and picking off one running person after another. I thought of Jenna first, but I didn't have time for a second thought.

A police siren pierced the air and the man tossed down one gun and pulled a new one out of a back holster. I was about a hundred yards away behind the wheel of the car and the circle of people that had once been around him was quickly dispersing. His back was to me as I saw him aim at the center of the back of one fleeing woman and fire.

That was when I made the decision.

I hammered the accelerator to the floor and the car lurched forward. The shooter must have registered the racing motor, but it was too late. He raised the gun and aimed for the center of my windshield, but the bullets entered the car on the passenger side. I ran him over as if he were a speed bump and immediately slammed on the brakes. I had seen his body fly high into the air and land behind me in a disfigured whirl of Army clothing. The car finally came to rest on the sidewalk just before crashing through the front door of the restaurant. I had taken down a street sign and glanced off a fire hydrant and two parked cars.

"Jesus, please! He was the only one I hit, please!" I cried.

I jumped out of the car and raced back towards the shooter. He was moving slowly, reaching for the gun that was just a few feet away. His right femur bone was sticking out of his pant leg. The mask was still covering his face. The police were on the way and I watched the red flashing lights approaching from every angle. But, I still needed to beat him to the gun.

As it turned out, it wasn't much of a battle. He grabbed the gun and raised it in my direction. A quick pull of the trigger sent me sprawling backwards and as I hit the sidewalk, everything I knew ran through my mind all at once.

CHAPTER 13

*"As a well-spent day brings happy sleep,
so a life well-used brings happy death."*
Leonardo DaVinci

I was out for three days. Evidently, the bullet pierced my right side and just kept right on going, but it had done some damage. The shot had not entered my abdominal cavity, which was terrific news, but the muscle it had torn through was a mess. Immediate surgery preceded an infection that had to be quickly controlled, but still, I opened my eyes to a dark room, a rancid smell, and the beeps from the machines hooked to my body through one port or another. I had no idea where I was or how I had arrived there, but for one reason or another I was thinking about death. As I lay there, awake for the first time in days, I thought of a funeral I had attended in my hometown. A young woman had died from injuries suffered in a one-car accident. She died too young.

With my eyes finally open, I was thrilled to realize that my brain was also working. I thought of the moment when I had sent the shooters body spiraling through the air, and it all came rushing back to me. A loud, piercing scream shattered the silence of the hospital corridor, and the pounding in my head begged for someone to make the screams stop, but they continued. It was a loud, siren-like scream that just went on and on, and despite the fact that I suddenly realized that I was in a trauma center, there had to be someone around who could attend to the screaming fool, didn't there?

All at once, my room filled with three or four rushing bodies.

"Stop the screaming!" I cried out.

"Sal!" the woman on the right called out. She was dressed in scrubs with a blue and red flower pattern. "Sal, you're the one who's screaming," she whispered.

***

I needed answers. The screaming had stopped, but the urge to scream was ever-present. I asked for those answers and the middle-aged, over-worked nurse with the slight limp from being on her feet for ten hours every day was quick to respond.

"The police want to speak with you as does every news outlet across the nation. You were a hero, Sal. You were a true hero. You saved a lot of lives."

"I'm concerned about three lives," I said.

I struggled to get to a seated position but the nurse would have none of it. Her strawberry blonde hair was most likely the result of a recent dye-job. Her heavy hands lowered me back to the bed. She smelled of antiseptic and the gloved hand was insistent.

"There are people who want to see you. Elaine is waiting to talk to you. She's been here every day."

So, Elaine was alive. Of course she was. It would take more than a sniper rifle to bring her down.

"Is Valerie with her?

The nurse did not give anything away.

"How is Jenna? Is Jenna all right?

Her face betrayed her with the mention of Jenna's name, but she remained quiet about it. In a flash, it occurred to me that Jenna was gone.

"Jenna's dead?" I asked.

"Please, Sal, just stay put for a minute," she whispered. "I will get someone to speak with you. You're a real popular guy."

There were flowers and gifts all over that lonely room. Had I killed the shooter? I know that I had stopped him long enough to get him arrested. I remembered the first responders on the scene, but who was saved was less important than who was still alive in my life.

The nurse wasn't even to the door before it opened. Two men in very expensive suits entered the room. They stopped at the foot of the bed. As if they practiced it, they flashed their badges. I simply glanced at them.

"We owe you a world of thanks," he said. "You ran down an active shooter and saved a lot of lives."

"How many died?" I asked.

"Eleven," the dark-haired, muscle-bound man in the dark suit answered. "Including Jenna."

The wave of grief that had been building inside of me threatened to spread over me. The love of my life had died.

"Valerie?" I asked.

"Valerie was wounded, but her injuries are not life-threatening. I also believe that you were there with Elaine, Valerie's mother."

"Yes," I said.

"She was uninjured, and a lot of men and women were able to walk away from that scene, uninjured because you acted. You're a hero to a number of families, and we owe you a mountain of thanks."

The pain in my abdomen suddenly reappeared, but it was no match for how I was feeling in the center of my chest. No matter how many times I repeated it in my mind, *Jenna's dead,* I couldn't make it stick.

"Can I see Valerie?" I asked.

"She's facing her own medical fight," the other guy said. He was also in a dark suit, but he was a tad shorter and his hair was blonde. "Valerie was hit in the face."

I attempted to sit up again, but the pain tore me back down.

"She was shot in the face? Who the fuck did this?"

The dark-haired agent took over.

"His name was Albert David Fordham. He was a lone wolf out to prove his worth. We discovered that he had a lifetime of mental problems."

"You think?" I shouted. "What tipped it off for you?"

The agents stood before me with bowed heads. I imagined that they were used to such despair.

"Is he dead, at least? Can you tell me if he's dead?"

"He will survive," the blonde guy said. "He's busted up to be sure, but he will survive. You have our word that he will pay for this."

"It doesn't matter, does it?"

Both men looked a bit confused by my question.

"We get rid of him, right, but how do we stop it from happening again tomorrow, in a different city, to different innocent people? Can you *fucking* stop it from happening again?"

Both sets of eyes were positioned to stare at the floor of the hospital room.

"We have a number of eyewitness accounts, but we need your story," the dark-haired guy said. "Will you let us know when you're ready to speak?"

I simply nodded. We all understood that just then was not a good time.

"Are you up for a visit from Elaine?"

"Of course I am," I said.

The two men headed for the door. Almost as if they were a dance team they turned back and addressed me once more.

"We appreciate what you did. You saved lives."

"But I didn't save Jenna," I said. "Jenna is gone."

***

I half-expected that they would wheel Elaine in to my bedside, but then it occurred to me that she gave holy hell to anyone that might treat her like an old lady. Instead, she walked right in.

"It's about time," she said. "I thought you were gonna' sleep forever."

I hadn't expected less of an entrance from Elaine, but as she got closer to the bed I saw it; for the first time she looked defeated, and old. Elaine looked like an elderly, sick woman.

Elaine moved to the right side of my bed and I slid my ass down the sheet in an attempt to bring myself forward. She pressed on my chest, ever so slightly, to push me back to the pillow.

"Stay where you are," she said.

Then she leaned in and kissed me on the lips before sitting down in the chair beside the bed.

"You stink," she said.

I actually thought about laughing, but of course, I couldn't.

"How's Val?" I asked. "And the baby! Jesus, how's the baby?"

A long pause led way to a heavy sigh and Elaine nodded.

"They're both going to be fine," she said. Tears filled her tired, old eyes. "Valerie took a shot in the mouth. It's a wonder it didn't kill her, and she's an absolute mess right now, but she'll survive. She'll be all right. They're watching the baby, but so far everything seems to be okay."

Elaine placed both of her hands over my right hand.

"I'm so sorry about Jenna," she said. "Sal, I can't even begin to express how much I grieve for that beautiful girl."

We simply sat there for a long time, in that pose. We didn't need to say anything more. I didn't need to know how it all happened. I didn't want a blow-by-blow accounting of every bullet that left those rifles. We simply sat there thinking about the loss of life, and our shattered hearts. Finally, I broke the silence.

"Why would God let this happen?" I asked.

"Come on!" Elaine said. "I've taught you better than that! It wasn't God, dummy. You'll figure that out."

But God was the culprit in my eyes. God had created Albert David Fordham. As sure as God was responsible for the good in the world, He had also created the bad.

"I'm going to get you a pad and pen soon," Elaine said. "You'll work to make some sense of it."

What's A Life Worth?

The line stretched out the door and snaked down the sidewalk. Person after person standing in the cold January air to pay their respects to a woman whose physical life came to an abrupt halt.

The town felt comfortable to me as I shook hands with people who I hadn't seen in quite some time. The faces looked worn, there was a considerable limp to the gathering as our eyes darted down and away, scared to say how lousy we felt for a strong family whose members we'd known since we were children.

I thought about the fact that there is a great debate going on in our nation as people speak of their rights to have and hold their guns. That's an argument for someone else, I'm done with it, but what captures me now is the thought of death, and how every single digit in the accounting of who died from what comes with a story.

"The stats are wrong," someone texted me. "There aren't 30,000 deaths from gun violence. There are 'only' 17,000."

In the context of standing on line to pay my respects, the 'only' 17,000 was lost on me.
My mind shifted to that little town in Connecticut and the endless parade of wakes and verses of 'Amazing Grace'.
The same sort of scene will repeat itself in Baltimore, and sadly might then move on to the next town. Somewhere here in America.

And I spoke a lot and wrote a lot about life being a gift and that it is meant to be lived with the tears, the smiles, and the work, and the play, and the filling of empty spaces with moments of love.
The full catastrophe of it all.
But mostly, I was feeling love.

Just love.

We forget the love when we throw out a statement like:

"More people die in car accidents; shall we ban cars."

We forget the gift when we mention that the majority of those shootings are inner-city, gang kids.

As if their lives are disposable.

We forget our faith when we pass judgment on folks who are looking for assistance to survive.

We chase away thoughts of compassion when we talk about the 'worthless' people who are trying to cross the border to find opportunity.

And I realize that my heart bleeds for others and that I take a lot of flack for it from folks who don't quite get feeling pain for someone that they might consider not worthy.

Life is a gift, but it is not just a gift for you. It's a gift for all of us. It's a gift that doesn't make mention of how much money is earned, or how smart one fancies themselves to be.

It's just a gift, and we are all entitled to share in it, and we shouldn't decide whose gift ends when or why. None of us are truly quite as disposable as one might think.

I got back into my car and made all the small turns around the neighborhoods of my small hometown. I crossed the street where I was tossed from my bike with my buddy Jeff following close behind. We could've been killed right there.

I drove past the spot where the shortstop for my softball team DID lose his life. I eased past my buddy Al's childhood home. I thought of his Mom and Dad, and how hard I cried at their funerals.

I felt warmed and comforted in the arms of that little town on a dark, unseasonably warm night.

"What took you so long?" my girlfriend chided me when I returned home.

"There were a lot of people there," I said.

"There aren't a lot of people in the whole town!" She said.

"But they all feel it," I said. "They all appreciate the pain. They all show up because they know life is tough. They show their love."

So as we discuss all the issues that confront us on the streets of a whole bunch of small towns I pray that we remember:

Every life is a gift.

Every one of those numbers means something to hundreds and hundreds and hundreds of people.

Perhaps when we value one another...

Perhaps when we value one another.

CHAPTER 14

*"Sir, my concern is not whether God is on our side;
my greatest concern is to be on God's side,
for God is always right."*
Abraham Lincoln

The next couple of weeks passed in a flurry of absolute physical and mental anguish. Whenever I closed my eyes I pictured Jenna in my mind as though her life had been a movie that I had taped for constant viewing. I saw her as a mother, a lover, a crazed woman, and a superstar. I recalled her in sickness, in health, laughing and crying. The replay of the woman that she had been, rushed into my brain, and played like a film on a reel. I cried for what I lost, but I also cried for the love that we all lost. I wasn't even able to attend the four memorial services that were held for her in three different cities.

The television news stories were running wild with the story. Every piece of footage that they had of Jenna as an actress was played over and over. The reporters spoke of the 'senseless tragedy' and treated her days as more important than the days of the other ten people who had been gunned down. There was hardly ever a mention of those who had been injured with the possible exception of me. I was a hero. I deserved all the accolades.

I couldn't watch much of the coverage and I had left explicit instructions with my editor, John Paige, that I was off-limits to all media. Paige was happy to handle it for me as long as I gave him the exclusive when I felt up to it.

"You know what your problem is?" Elaine asked.

She was seated at my bedside working a crossword puzzle from a huge book of puzzles that magnified the page so that she could actually see it. She had been splitting her time between my bedside, Valerie's bedside, and home with Max. I had no idea how she was accomplishing all of it, but I was sort of afraid to ask.

"What's that?" I asked.

"You spend a lot of time trying to repair the devastation in life that you're incapable of fixing," Elaine said.

I struggled to sit up. The doctors were making noise about letting me return home in a day or so, and the moment when I got out of bed couldn't come soon enough. I had been taking short walks up and down the hospital corridor, but I was just about done with all of this.

"Is that right?" I asked, knowing that she was a hundred percent right.

"Of course it is," she said. "Every day of your life, for better or worse, is a constant struggle of you attempting to defeat it. You're chasing windmills."

I reached for the bottle of water on the table to my right. The pain was still ever-present in my abdomen, but movement really sent shivers to my brain. Elaine didn't budge in an effort to help me get the water.

"Is all of that there in your crossword book?" I asked.

"It's right here in my noggin'," Elaine said as she tapped the left side of her head with her index finger.

"So, what do I do about it?" I asked.

"Well, you'll probably run in a circle until your heart gives way," she said. "You ain't all that bright."

I smiled.

"Yet, sonny boy, the moment that you truly arrive in this life is the moment when you figure out that hope is just pure folly. Life drains the hope out of you, but you gotta' go on anyway."

Elaine coughed up a huge ball of phlegm. She spit it into a napkin.

"Well, isn't all that lovely?" I asked. "Not only do you dash all hope, but you utterly destroy all my faith by spitting into the only napkin I have left in the world."

Elaine laughed. She closed the puzzle book and took a long while to lift herself up and out of the chair.

"I gave you plenty to think about. I have to go see Valerie, get my titties zapped, take the dog outside, and go to bed. If you ever decide to get up off your ass maybe you can help me with some of that."

Elaine leaned into the bed and kissed me quickly.

"You're amazing," I said.

"No shit," she responded. "And while you're thinking about all the pain in your heart, think about that. That's what life is. I'm what love is."

Elaine shuffled to the hospital door. She was just about to yank it open when it opened for her and a man dressed in a thousand dollar suit stepped through.

"Salvatore Pisceo?" the man asked.

"Do I *look* like a Salvatore?" Elaine asked. "He's the lump under the covers."

Elaine stepped into the hallway and my visitor stepped forth. The man didn't even have to open his mouth for me to understand what was going on. Jenna hadn't left the world without being prepared for that eventuality.

It didn't take long for the man to get straight to the point.

"Mr. Pisceo, I'm Claude Reynolds, Jenna's attorney."

Reynolds extended a hand to me and I shook it quickly.

"Just after the murder of her husband, Jenna called to us with a request to change her will, in particular the guardianship of Tyler, which she has awarded to you."

I thought of Valerie and the child growing inside of her. I considered that we were both badly injured. Was I ready for the massive responsibility of caring for two children? The gravity of it all weighed down heavily on my shoulders. Yet how could I refuse? We had once had a child together that we had lost. Jenna, in her death, was returning a son to me.

Reynolds held an accordion briefcase on his hip and he sifted through papers and pushed them forward for me to sign. He seemed a bit nervous about the task at hand as if I were about to tell him to disappear and keep the child where he was.

"Given the present circumstances, of course, we don't expect to just leave Tyler with you. Tyler has a nanny in New York and he is receiving excellent care, but Jenna wished for you to raise him from this point forward."

"Of course," I said. "But it may be a little while before I can get settled."

"I understand."

I glanced at a few of the papers. There were little yellow post-its in place for my signature.

"I can leave those with you," he said, "and there is no hurry."

Reynolds stood before me, nervously moving from one leg to the next.

"That's fine," I said. "I will love Tyler as if he were my own. Of course, I will."

"There's one other thing," Reynolds said.

Another sheaf of papers appeared out of his briefcase.

"Jenna also left a sizeable trust fund for Tyler in the amount of $4.2 million dollars. You are the guardian of the trust fund until he reaches the age of 18. The rest of her estate was also left to you, and there's a little over three million dollars there. The home was in her husband's name and is currently left in his family, as were the family automobiles and properties. There may eventually be an additional cash payout involved with the settlement of additional items."

Reynolds also pushed those papers forward for my consideration.

"She took good care of you," he said. "She truly loved you."

The words were no sooner out of his mouth when the tears just exploded from deep inside. I doubled over as the cost of suddenly exploding in heart pain seemed to tear at my insides where the bullet had invaded me.

"I'm very sorry for your loss," Reynolds was saying as he was backpedaling towards the door. "Jenna was a beautiful woman."

For a long time after he left I stared at the door where Reynolds had escaped. All of it came crashing down on my head and the reality of being shot, and losing Jenna, and worrying about Valerie was just too much for me. The tears blasted out of me as if someone had flipped a switch, and I immediately thought about God, because when everything else is stripped away, that's all that's truly left. When the world rips you up, you have to go to a higher authority, I suppose.

The prayers that I offered were more accusatory than anything else. I didn't want Jenna's money. I truly only wanted Jenna. I didn't want to be hailed a hero for running down a man who was hurting others. I only wanted the hurting to stop.

"Why is there so much pain?" I wailed. "Why God do you leave us here not knowing anything at all about what it takes to live with pain?"

Valerie was in another hospital somewhere recovering from her gunshot. Elaine had updated me every single step of the way, but I had no control, and no idea how she was handling her hefty portion of the misery. The shot had knocked out eleven teeth. The bullet fragments would forever remain embedded in her broken jaw. She'd already endured three surgeries and there were at least three more to come.

"The surgeon says that in a few months you won't even know that she'd ever been shot," Elaine had said.

Elaine carried my daily messages to Valerie, and returned each day with Valerie's own declarations of devotion. Yet it would be a long walk back to what we had been building. The pain would manifest itself in so many days ahead.

"God make me stronger than the pain," I cried. "Please, God, please."

***

Everything I Know About Living Broken-Hearted

The pain comes out of nowhere some days. It tears at your heart, and since it is controlled by the mind, the physical pain that it causes it most confusing, but it's real. Yet when you tabulate the data at the end of any life well-lived, the pain is present because the love was once there, and when love is ripped away, pain soon follows. Yet there comes a moment, in the middle of the hurt, when reality sets in, and you understand that you have to live with it. You won't ever like it, but you need to get on with it all. To dwell on what was lost will simply double the pain. You can't chase the windmills. You can't fix the devastation, but you can certainly build upon the foundation of what is left.

I knew a woman who lived her life filled with the excitement of just being alive. She was beautiful in every sense of the word. She wasn't perfect, of course, but she was life personified. She'd show you rage. She'd laugh so heartily that you'd think she was on the verge of hurting herself, and then she'd cry big tears that would roll down her angelic face and fall at her feet. She lived completely. She loved thoroughly. It was just impossible to realize that she could ever be taken away. She was too much of a force to be forever gone, and she isn't, of course, but the gale-force winds of grace and beauty that she blew into my life are now just soft breezes on a cold day.

How do you live broken-hearted?

You must find a way to feel those strong winds every day, in some way because no one ever completely leaves. The spirit is left behind. The love doesn't go away. It's given to the universe, and on the moments when it all seems so utterly useless to carry on, the universe will give some of that love back to you.

I'll love you, forever, Jenna. I'll hold it tightly. I'll treasure the cool breeze. I'll cherish the pain I feel because it's proof that you were right here; in my broken heart.

CHAPTER 15

*"The mystery of human existence lies in not
just staying alive, but in finding something to live for."
Fydor Dostoyevsky*

I hadn't laid eyes on Valerie since I left the restaurant to get the car. Seventeen days later I used a walker to enter her hospital room as one of the nurses held the door open for me. Elaine was at the side of the bed, of course, and she stood up quickly as I entered.

"I don't even want you to look at me," Valerie said with a cry in her voice.

"You're the most beautiful sight I've ever seen," I said as my own voice cracked.

"You both look like holy hell," Elaine said, but the sing-song quality of her voice was just what we needed to send us into the tight embrace. I kissed tears off Valerie's eyes.

"You saved our lives," she said. "He was going to kill us all. He killed Jenna."

I tried to quiet Valerie with soft kisses, but the words were stuck in my throat. There wasn't any way that I could make it better for her.

"Oh God, what do we do to survive this?" Valerie asked.

"We just do," I said.

I opened my arms and invited Elaine into our embrace.

"He's right," Elaine said. "We just do."

***

As I sat in the hard brown chair beside Valerie's bed we tackled a variety of painful discussions. Of course the most important of all was that the baby was still safe. Valerie didn't much care that her face was a mess, she only worried about the life growing inside her, but she also found compassion for me. We held one another, as much as we could, and we cried together. People often dream of making love, and sharing the wonderful moments in life, but being able to cry on one another's shoulders might be even more powerful. I couldn't have possibly held her any tighter than I did during those first few hours. I grew hoarse from telling her how much I loved her, but she also knew that my love for Jenna, while being different, was equally as powerful.

"Can you make peace?" Valerie whispered in the dark of that hospital room. I was leaning out of the chair, holding her hand, trying to make out the beauty of her face behind the heavy bandages. We were in the dark, and we were horrifically damaged.

"Love isn't finite," I said. "Love doesn't have limits, and it can't be taken from me."

Yet I cried as Valerie's index fingers made circles in the palm of my hand. Her simple touch, and the ache in her whisper as she spoke, validated it for me.

"As long as there's *you*…as long as there's *me*," I whispered.

***

I'm not quite sure why it was so important to me, but on the first night home in my bed I was overwhelmed with the thought that I needed to be up in time to see the sun rise again. Max wasn't even bothering with the end of the bed. His head was right beside mine. We were practically sharing a pillow. He looked at me quizzically as I turned out the light and then cried softly in the dark. I could feel his big eyes on me, and it forced me into a thought that would propel me forward.

"The sun is going to rise in the morning," I whispered.

Max flicked his huge pink tongue in the direction of my face and I didn't turn away. I laughed.

That's what life is, I thought. *Life was simply the never ending belief that somehow it just might work and that you can someday laugh again.*

I groped for my phone and checked the time for the sun rise. I set my alarm for twenty minutes before it was supposed to begin its climb.

"I hope it still comes up, Maxy-boy," I said.

Max slowly lowered his sizeable head and closed his eyes. The light from my phone dimmed. Max was content. I was going have to figure out how to be.

***

The next morning, the pain in my mid-section was pretty much a living, breathing thing and I opened my eyes before the alarm even signaled that it was time to get the hell up again.

The sun was about to rise.

Jenna wouldn't be seeing it this morning.

I struggled to the bathroom with my right hand pressed tight against my stomach. I scrounged around in the medicine cabinet for the pain killers that the doctors had prescribed for me.

We spend half our adult lives just trying to get the pain to subside.

I thought of Valerie in the hospital bed, half her mouth shot off, a baby forming inside her. I thought of Elaine and her cancer treatments to keep death at bay.

We're all just trying to live, one more day, to see the sun rise.

I couldn't recall the last time that I'd actually looked at the rising sun. I gobbled up two of the pills, took a sip of water, and with Max at my heels headed for the kitchen and the waiting pot of coffee. The delayed brew had filled the pot for me as I slept. Max did a little dance at the back door as I filled my cup.

The light on my phone was blinking incessantly. I hadn't bothered to answer the phone since the shooting. Everyone wanted to speak to me. Every reporter in the country had evidently tried to reach me. I had sent all inquiries to the paper and to John Paige. I smiled thinking about what a living hell his life must be as he waited for me to respond.

Everyone wants the ugly story.

It was sort of ironic, but I had dedicated my career writing columns that begged people to live the right way and it was a mass shooting with many casualties that was going to turn me into the man-of-the-month across the nation. I found it all so silly. I just wanted to watch the sun come up.

I opened the back door and Max exploded out into the yard.

I sat on a lawn chair and sipped the coffee, raising my eyes to the sky above. I watched the flight of a robin, following him to a low-hanging branch on my neighbor's apple tree. The bird wasn't singing, rather, it was making an almost growling sound that was strange to me. Before too long it got sick of its spot and headed elsewhere, away from me. The sun, on the other hand, was steady. The sky was clear and the rising sun brought a feeling of hopefulness to my heart. The thought of death was going to slowly kill me if I let it, and I considered something that my father had told me long ago.

Sorrow will come for you, Dad had said.

But Dad had also added something else.

Better let some of the beauty in.

The rising sun was beautiful. I looked straight at it, holding my left hand on my forehead as a visor. Max was busy investigating every inch of the grass, lifting his leg everywhere it appeared that he had to.

Max appeared right in front of me and I patted his head.

"What if this is all there is, buddy?" I asked. "What if Jenna is just gone?"

Max took my questions as an invitation to join me in my seat and he placed his huge paws on my legs and hoisted himself up until we were face-to-face.

"Think of all the things I don't know," I said. "When everything you do know…turns to shit."

Everything I Know About Deconstructing

We begin our lives as blank slates. Little by little, we learn. We learn how to stand, how to walk and how to eventually run. Moment by moment we start putting together a plan. We try to improve every single day, hopefully, in all kinds of ways. Our golf score gets better because we take a lesson or two. Our relationships grow because we learn of understanding, and trust and commitment. We live our lives in a never-ending quest to learn, and that is if we are doing it right.

Yet there comes a moment when we tip to the other side. The scales go out of balance and we start to go the other way. There was a time when I wanted to become the greatest baseball player in the history of the world. As a little league player I figured out what it took to stand in the batter's box and not be afraid. Soon enough I figured out that I could get a single to right field if I just went the way that the ball was pitched. I started running faster, playing smarter, hitting the ball further and further. Other players started to recognize my strengths, and then opponents started to expose my weaknesses. For a long, long, long time I thought about the fact that I was getting better. My expectations had changed, but along the way I had turned myself into a fairly good player, and then time tipped the scales.

I remember the moment well. There were two on and two out in the last inning and I was playing the field, at second base. The pop-up was directly behind me. My mind shifted to the thought that the game was over. I had trained my legs to move. I had taught my eyes to judge the trajectory of the ball, and I raced towards the ball, just knowing that I'd made hundreds of such catches as I'd grown as a player.

But the ball was falling to the ground more quickly than my legs could get me there. It landed in the grass in right field as I tumbled towards the ground, not believing that I just hadn't made it. In the end, it didn't matter much, it was just a recreation league game, and the beer was still cold in the bar after.

"Getting old," a teammate said to me. "We're no longer getting better. Now we're getting worse."

It seems to me that there is a tipping point in life as well. We strive and strive and strive and strive, but eventually, it seems that it's all we can do. We're slowly deconstructing, and the world that we live in eventually breaks down completely. That is everything I know about getting worse.

CHAPTER 16

"You can't shut off the risk and the pain
without losing the love that remains."
Bruce Springsteen

I simply had no choice in the matter anymore. I was going to have to return John Paige's call. I grabbed my cell phone, searched for his name and punched in the number. He answered before the first ring even finished.

"You ready?" he asked.

"I'm fine, John, how are you?" I asked.

"Sorry, buddy. How *are* you? You okay?"

I almost laughed at the question.

"No. How would you be okay?" He asked. "I'm sorry again."

I decided to let John wiggle off the hook.

"I'll talk to Katie Couric," I said. "I'll do one interview. Then I want some time to try and figure out if I even want to write anymore."

John was quiet for a long moment. I envisioned him searching the contact book for Katie Couric's direct number.

"I know you're gonna' write," he said. "You're a writer. You have to tell us what you know."

"Not sure I know a fucking thing."

We went over the particulars. The interview wouldn't happen until tomorrow morning as I still needed time to process it all. Eleven people had died. Fourteen people were battling to get whole again. There was a chance that some of those who were injured would not survive.

"I don't mean to sound crass," John said, "but the news cycles fast. You know that. The story is still alive, but people will soon forget. You need to bring Jenna's death to life."

I lifted the shade to look out my front window. The news trucks were lining the streets in front of my home. I had ducked all of them, but they were waiting patiently. I leaned across my couch and watched those men and women, in front of my home. They were sipping coffee. They were talking to one another. Channels 2, 4 and 7 were all out there, just waiting. They had waited for 17 days!

Max joined me on the couch and he placed his huge paws over the back of the couch and nudged the blind with his nose. The sudden movement of the blind sent some of the reporters scrambling for their cameras and I couldn't help but laugh.

Yet, the sudden flurry also sent my mind racing.

Why did these people want to speak to me?

I couldn't help those who were suffering because a madman had decided not to play by the rules of society anymore.

What words could I say to soothe anyone's shattered heart?

"It's all shit!" I cried out, and Max turned his wet nose to me. He nudged me with his wet nose and I pulled him close as the vultures on the street tried to snap a picture.

I had never felt more worthless in my entire life.

Yet Max was showing me his love.

***

I didn't even bother trying to sneak out. I simply walked out into my driveway and climbed into Valerie's car and with a wave of reporters making a charge at me I backed out of my driveway, knowing that they would get out of my way.

"WHEN WILL YOU TALK?" was the basic question that was being shouted at me.

I lowered the driver's side window.

"Just one more day, please," I said.

That apparently wasn't good enough because the reporters made a surge towards the car. Their voices filled my ears, but I couldn't make out even a single question. I simply had no ability to decipher words. I was on my way to pick up Elaine to take her for her treatment and then off to the hospital to visit Valerie and my baby. It was all that mattered.

As I drove away I couldn't help but be blinded by the brightness of the sun in the same blue sky.

Everything is still the same even though nothing is, I thought. *Everything is the same even though nothing ever will be again.*

There were also a couple of reporters waiting at Valerie and Elaine's home. I employed the same strategy in dealing with them as I parked the car and bolted for the front door. Elaine swung the door open and stepped out quickly with her mouth already in full gear.

"Back the fuck off!" She yelled. "Or I'm gonna' smash you with my cane!"

I knew better than to reach for Elaine. I sensed that the beautiful news anchor from Channel 2 also knew that approaching Elaine wouldn't be wise. As she ambled to the car the reporter backed away knowing that she would not get even a single sentence that they could use. When we were safely in the car I said the very first thing that came to mind.

"Do you realize how unbelievably beautiful you are?" I asked.

"Shut the hell up," Elaine said. "Get me to the doctor."

She turned her face away from me in an effort to hide her tears, but I saw them clearly.

"I can't believe there's so much evil," she whispered.

***

As Elaine went to her treatment I sat in an isolated room, clear of the other people who were waiting on their loved one. I had requested the room because there were way too many people simply staring at me, pointing and whispering, or worse yet...looking for my autograph or even a photo. It was way too weird.

I sat alone in a room that had a small table and two hard plastic chairs. I was thinking of what I might say on television tomorrow and my thoughts were just way too jumbled up. I kept seeing Jenna's face in my mind. I could hear her laughter in my head. I was going to have to block all of that out if I was going to survive this. At the moment when I came to that conclusion there was a soft knock on the door.

"Sal, can I talk to you about Elaine?" Dr. Toni Wilson's blonde hair was tightly wrapped in a bun on her head and her tight expression told me that something was seriously amiss. She held a clipboard tight to her chest, but she didn't look down or hide her eyes. She stared right at me.

"Yes, what's wrong?" I started to stumble out of my seat but she settled me down with a hand motion. She then sat in the chair directly across from me.

"Are you aware that this is her final treatment?" She asked.

"I did **not** know that," I said. "Things have been strange."

The woman nodded. She was most likely the only woman in the world who was too busy to care that I had run down a mass murderer. Either that or she had been all through it with Elaine. Either way, she was all business now.

"Elaine doesn't want to hear anything about extending her treatments. I've explained to her that we can be sure that all of the cancer is gone if she'll go through radiation for another month or so. She's also saying that she's not going to pay the three hundred dollar fee for the medication that she needs. She said: 'That's it! Done with this shit! They're making me dizzy anyway.'"

I might have smiled had the situation not caught me so off-guard. Elaine had never once resisted any treatment. She wanted to get better. She knew what she had to do.

"I'll talk to her," I said.

"She's a tough lady," Dr. Wilson said. "But she needs to extend the treatment plan."

"I understand that."

Dr. Wilson was on her feet and moving to the door. She turned around slowly.

"I can't even pretend to know how badly you're hurting," she said, "but I wanted to say that you did a great thing."

It was going to be really rough getting ready for the Katie Couric interview. I had no idea how to respond to Dr. Wilson. I could only bow my head.

Elaine didn't want to hear anything to the contrary. We were going to Denny's no matter how many people wanted to shake my hand.

"I'll keep them away from the table," she said.

We were settled in the car and instead of turning the key, I turned to face Elaine.

"What in the hell do you think you're doing?" I asked.

"She told you after I told her not to?" Elaine asked.

"It's not about her," I said. "It's about you. What makes you think I'm going to let you stop now?"

Elaine wouldn't even look at me. Her left hand was trembling, but I knew better than to touch her, but I did. She let me.

"I can't believe it," she said.

There were tears in her voice. She kept her head turned away, but she repositioned her arm so that she could grab my hand. Her tiny, bony, worn hand held mine.

"I know that life is miserable, but look at you. You lost a son and an ex-wife. Valerie is in a bed with a baby depending on her as she recovers from gunshot wounds to the face. No one gives a flying fuck about anyone else anymore. We're living a fucking soap opera! It's easier to quit, isn't it?"

I let the question hang in the air for a long moment, and then I got pissed.

"Are you kidding me right now?"

Elaine's body was rocked by the sob that she fought so hard to hold in.

"Seriously? *You're* quitting? You think I'm going to *let* you quit?"

Unbelievably there were two reporters making their way towards the car.

"Look at them," Elaine said. "Running to us to try and get a good shot of the devastation."

It was a young woman with a bearded man with a camera high in the air. I started the engine and gunned it, as they say, racing to the busy street. I cut out into traffic, leaving them to snap shots of the ass-end of my truck.

"I really need you," I said. "Valerie really needs you. Your grandchild is waiting to meet you."

Elaine didn't answer. She let go of my hand.

"Will you continue your treatments?" I asked.

"I don't want to live angry or scared," she said.

"Then don't," I answered. "But you *gotta* live."

She took another moment to gather her unbelievable strength.

"I want a ham and cheese melt," she said.

"So do I," I said.

***

Everything I Know About Love

We need to feel love from the very moment that we take our first breath of air. We chase love all of our natural lives. Love is just as essential as the food and water that we need to survive. Love is not easily attainable, but it comes in many forms. We feel the love of our parents, who protect us and nurture us. We come to depend upon the love of our siblings, knowing that we are chasing what we need to survive. As we grow we continue to chase love. We need companionship. We thirst for a sense of community. We hopefully build a life where we are able to surround ourselves with love. We bathe in the light that love brings. In our lives eventually we also gather darkness that threatens the light at nearly every single turn. Somehow we lose our focus on what it takes to gather love. If we allow it to happen we can somehow end up in a place where we are somehow simply surrounded by darkness. Life can beat us down. Sadness can leave us alone in the dark, groping for the light of love, but too tired to even crawl to somehow get back there again. Love is overcoming the darkness. Love is sharing the laughter that we are blessed with in a heart that needs light. Love is the feeling of running through fields of gold on a perfect summer day. Love is holding a child in our arms and listening to their cry. Love is touching the hand of someone you simply love. Love is life and life is love and even in death love will eventually win. Love is not giving in. Love is faith. Love is hope. Love is strength. It's not all we need, but it's certainly exactly what we do need. And that's Everything I Know About Love.

CHAPTER 17

*"The best and most beautiful things in this world
cannot be seen or even heard, but must be
felt with the heart."*
Helen Keller

Before the interview even started the lights were getting to me.
Katie Couric was whispering words of encouragement to me, but
I couldn't quite get over the fact that the lights were so bright and
that she was seated right beside me. Elaine was just feet away in
the front row, but I found that if I looked her way I might actually
lose it. The cameraman did a bit of a countdown and before I knew
it, I was live on television in what was being billed as an 'exclusive
interview with a hero.'

"Good evening," Katie said. "We're here tonight to speak with Sal
Piseco, the hero of the awful, latest mass murder in this country that
left eleven people dead, including actress Jenna Powers. There were
also fourteen injured, including three seriously."

Katie turned to me and I absolutely froze under the glaring lights.
I stammered out a "Hello." Katie must have noticed the panic
because she jumped right into the first question.

"What was going through your mind when you rounded the corner and saw the shooter?"

"Not much," I said. "Um, I heard the popping noise and the sad thing was that I thought of all the mass murders I'd heard about through the years. The people at those scenes always described the 'pop-pop-pop.' That was what registered."

Katie's face took on a look of grief. She placed her left hand on my right arm.

"The terror in such a situation is indescribable and you don't have much of a chance to make up your mind about what to do, right?"

"Split-second decision," I said. "I had to stop him. It was an easy decision"

I took a deep breath and all at once it occurred to me that I was going to be able to talk my way through it, but when Katie said Jenna's name, I nearly lost it.

"You were married to Jenna Powers and as the world knows you lost a child soon after birth. It was too much for your marriage, but you still loved her deeply, didn't you?"

"Love isn't a temporary thing," I said. "I certainly loved Jenna. I still do even though she's no longer here, but that's the fundamental difference between normal, living, loving breathing people like you or I, and a man like Albert David Fordham. Life and love is all about connecting, to something. In some way, somehow, we all need to feel a connection."

"Albert David Fordham," Katie said.

She pronounced his name slowly, allowing the disdain to drip off each syllable.

"We are producing way too many men like him."

This was why I was seated before Katie Couric and talking to millions of people. I glanced to Elaine in the audience and she flashed a determined look of love.

"Fordham is just twenty-two years old. He's spent the last seven years in and out of jail and therapy. His medical health records are sealed, but he lived in a trailer home in an abandoned trailer park. His makeshift home was guarded by an electric fence and signs that said he had closed circuit television that was monitoring activity around his property. He had a sign that said there was an attack dog on duty and one that said that 'due to the price of ammo there would be no warning shots.' He was outspoken on social media about his freedoms and how the white people of this nation needed to take their country back."

Katie was nodding along, her face a mask of absolute concern.

"And here's the kicker," I waited a long moment for the sentence to have the impact that I wanted it to have.

"Every single gun that he owned, and used to massacre all of those people, was one-hundred percent legally purchased."

Katie allowed the words to sink in.

"Surely the gun debate is raging," she said.

"I'm not blaming the gun," I said. "I'm blaming the rules that allow Fordham the freedom to arm himself in any way that he would like in a society that begs for politeness. He is a mentally ill human being and he was allowed to carry out his agenda of hate by owning weapons that are dangerous even in the most responsible of hands."

Katie agreed, of course, but she knew that what I was saying was exactly what she needed me to say to draw people to the interview and grab one sentence after another to play on their own newscasts.

"What do we do?" Katie said.

"Absolutely nothing," I answered.

I let it all hang in the air for as long as I could.

"We just pray that the next one doesn't involve another loved one, but make no mistake, there's another one coming. I guess we just hope and pray that it doesn't happen in our town again."

"There must be something that we can do, as a society, to someday eliminate such pain," Katie said.

"Of course there is, but we won't do it," I said. "It's too hard to make the changes necessary. Yet I'd like to try and make it come alive, a little bit, for all of you. I lost someone that I loved. After a nice dinner, as she waited for the car to pick her up, in front of the restaurant, a mentally ill man decided that her life, and the life of so many other people, wasn't worth anything. Now I've always appreciated the gift of life...not just my life...but the life of the man or woman right beside me on the bus, or subway, or airplane. You want to talk about rights? We all have the right to live our lives free of being gunned down like deer. Jenna was a wild celebration of life. She didn't always do everything right. She may have been a little selfish, but she was beautiful, and not just physically beautiful. Like all the people killed or injured that day her beauty was simply dependent upon her love of life and her fellow man. She just loved the fact that the sun rose in the sky each day. She loved walking in the rain, and singing her favorite song. Jenna loved being in love with her son, Tyler. She was crazy, mad, impulsive, loving, happy, sad, and miserable. She was all of those things because she was alive...and now she's not...and we won't do a single thing about the reason why she had to die here in the greatest country on Earth."

The faces of the dead were shown on the broadcast. Each man or woman slain was given a 60-second feature that recapped their days. Sixty seconds on a national show was all their lives amounted to that night.

As the interview wound down Katie thanked me for being brave. I did a very poor job of accepting her praise. I turned the tables on Katie by asking a single question.

"Katie, can you imagine living in a country where you will never again have to tell the world about a mass murder?"

She tilted her head to the left as if she did not understand the question.

"No," she said. "I will be reporting about it again, and again, and again and again."

I thought of Elaine telling me to look straight into the camera as I delivered the final line.

"These are people who are dying in the streets," I said. "People who want to live. These are men, women and children who shouldn't have to die."

I took the pregnant pause that Elaine had begged me to take and then delivered the final questions.

"Are we just going to accept this? Aren't we better than this? Can't we save our own citizens?"

Katie bowed her head. At that moment I honestly believe that she knew what an impossible problem we were there to discuss.

"I'm not a hero," I said. "I'm going to live the rest of my life with a profound sadness in my heart. These are people dying for no reason other than we can't figure out how to live."

PART II

CHAPTER 1 – JULY 2, 2014

"The purpose of our lives is to be happy."
Dalai Lama

We were just living.

Nearly two years had passed. Time passing is a funny thing. It's just seconds turning into minutes, into hours, into days, into weeks, into months and mercifully into years. The pain doesn't go away, but it changes. It becomes an almost tangible thing as you flip through the calendar of time that exists in your own head.

Max was on his last legs, almost literally. He spent most of the seconds of his day with his eyes closed. When it was time to eat, or go outside, or take a ride, Max would summon the energy and limp to the truck. I would, most of the time, have to lift him into the passenger seat, but he was certainly determined to take the trip around the block. Max wants to live, but how many minutes he has left is anyone's guess, just as it is for all of us.

"Are you going to help me in here?" Valerie's voice carried out into the backyard and it was as if she had pushed a button that made my legs come to life. I jumped out of the lounge chair and made a beeline for the kitchen. Valerie had the baby on her left hip and she somehow managed to point at the boiling pot of water on the stove.

"The potatoes are ready to be mashed and the roast is warming up in the oven. You need to slice it."

Seeing as how I had been cleaning up the dog shit in the back yard just before falling into the lounge chair, I thought it might be best to wash my hands before getting the food ready.

"I'm on it," I said.

Valerie held the baby up to me. Our baby, the child who showed me what life can be, cried out for me. I was suddenly struck by the beauty of it all. My wife and my child, Julianne Elaine, were both showing love on their faces. I must have hesitated in the moment because Valerie flashed a look of impatience, telling me, without a sound, that the potatoes were indeed boiling over.

"I love you," I said.

"Great!" she said, with a smile in her voice. "Get the potatoes! You know how my mother grades the quality of how they're mashed."

I turned to the stove and yelled out.

"Tyler! Mother! Dinner is ready!"

"Keep your pants on," Elaine said. "I'm schooling this boy in backgammon."

Moments later we were all seated at the table. Valerie, Tyler, Juli, Elaine and Elaine's oxygen tank. Max was at my feet, waiting for me to toss him a scrap or two.

"So, how was everyone's day?" Valerie asked, and the normal, routine, mundane, beautiful, wonderful, miraculous act of simply living was front and center.

***

By ten o'clock that night everything had settled down. Max was settled into the doggy bed on my side of the room and Valerie climbed in beside me. I set down the John Sandford book that I was nearly finished with and turned towards my wife.

"Are you over it?" she asked.

The question was directly out of left field, but I didn't need much of an explanation. I knew that she was speaking of the shooting, and more specifically Jenna's death. Still and all, 'over it' was a weird way to ask how I was doing.

"I'm sorry," Valerie said. "That was a stupid way to ask you how you're doing."

Valerie's hand went instinctively to her face. Even though there weren't any physical reminders of her pain as the plastic surgeons had done wonders, I was sure that her mental anguish was far from complete.

"There's no way over something like that," I said. "The other day I read that the average person has a better chance of being struck by lightning than being involved in a mass shooting."

"Doesn't seem that way anymore," Valerie said. "I hate that you told me that anyway because that is the type of thing someone who is trying to minimize the violence says. The death and the pain are real. Now that piece of crap is sitting in a cell somewhere and we are forced to get 'over it.'"

I didn't much want to rehash it all, but I knew that Valerie was asking me how I was doing for a reason. I needed to get 'over it' to get on with my life's work.

"I know you don't want to write the column anymore," she said, "but what about a book?"

The thought had crossed my mind, but I didn't know what the reason for a book would be. Jenna had left us plenty of money to take care of our little family. I had plenty to do as the cook, cleaner and as a Dad and caregiver for Elaine. I loved not worrying about much more than providing love and comfort, but we both knew that it wasn't enough.

I reached for Valerie's hand and she moved closer to me so that I could put an arm around her shoulder. Ever since the shooting, Valerie longed to be held, kissed, and just plain touched. She explained that she needed to feel contact. I was more than happy to provide it. We had cried ourselves to sleep on many nights, just touching our way through the pain.

"A book," I said. "I'll call it 'Changing Diapers, Cleaning Up Dog Shit and Being Berated by My Mother-In-Law.'"

Valerie laughed.

"Speaking of your mother-in-law, you know what she said to me today?"

"Heaven knows," I said.

"She said that she feels like this is her *last* year."

Elaine's health certainly was a concern to all of us, but I didn't even want to consider that she might be right. Elaine was the heartbeat of our home and she was almost solely responsible for Tyler adapting to what had been a horribly tragic life.

"I can't even think about that," I said, softly.

I caressed Valerie's shoulder and pulled her close. We shared a kiss and I watched a tear form in her right eye.

"It's going to happen," she said. "She beat cancer, but she's usually not wrong, you know."

"According to her she's never been wrong," I said, with a laugh. "She might be right about never being wrong too."

We both laughed.

"If I ever do write a book," I said. "I might just name it 'Elaine.'"

Valerie allowed the tear to race down her face without wiping it away. We had learned one simple thing since the shooting and that was to feel everything completely. Her smile was absolutely perfect, but her hand went instinctively to her jaw.

"The gift of life," I whispered.

"Yes, the gift of life," Valerie answered.

I felt my eyes getting a little droopy, but I also felt an unbelievable surge of love for the life that I was now leading.

"Tomorrow is Denny's day," I said. "Ham and cheese melt."

"She loves her weekly date with you so much," Valerie said. "Tyler has a baseball game on Legion Drive, when you two are done on your date we can all meet there."

"A perfect day," I said.

"The gift of life," Valerie whispered once more, and another day just faded away. We were living all of them to their fullest.

***

The next day, at exactly noon I angled the car into the parking lot at Denny's and I stopped at the front door to let Elaine out of the car. She had allowed me at least that concession. I still couldn't help her out of the car, mind you, but she did allow me to drop her at the door.

"I'm so fucking old," she said, with a laugh, but she struggled up and out of that seat. I watched her step out onto the sidewalk and use all of her strength to get to her feet.

"And it's a real mother-fucker," she added.

I laughed all the way to the parking spot.

The walk to the table seemed to take even more time. Elaine had a wheelchair at home, but she forbade me from using it for the trip to Denny's. Still and all, the waitress showed a touch of impatience as she waited for us to get seated. Susan held the menu close to her hip and Elaine caught the eye roll.

"Go serve that other table first, honey," she said. "We'll get settled. We aren't in a hurry."

Susan, to her credit, changed her approach. She waited for us to take the menus from her hand before leaving.

"Everyone's in such a damn hurry," Elaine said. "That's the biggest complaint I have about the world now. We used to have time for each other. I'm willing to be that she'll head to the back room and bitch to her coworkers that she's stuck serving the old lady."

"Ah, maybe she's nice," I said.

"Maybe," Elaine said. "But you'll see it when you get older. People lose their patience with you."

"I haven't lost patience with you," I said.

"No, you're exceptional."

Elaine didn't even bother with the menu and although I picked it up, I didn't need it either.

"I'm not gonna' make it another hundred days," Elaine said.

I just let the sentence sit there. I knew enough not to patronize her. Elaine's life could very easily be complete within a hundred days. Most days her breathing was labored and she would often fall asleep in the middle of a movie, or a meal, or a stroll around the backyard.

"Are you sad about it?" I asked.

Elaine laughed.

"I got my bags packed to go either way," she said. "But no, I'm not sad. How could I be? I've had a great life. It's been better than I could've imagined when you add it all up. I've had the pleasure of knowing you and Tyler."

Susan was nowhere to be found, but again, it didn't matter. We weren't in a hurry.

"You think there's life after death?" I asked.

"Of course there's life after death," she said. "I just ain't gonna' be in it."

It was my turn to laugh.

"But you *will* be here," I said. "You'll be with us."

Elaine's eyes closed and I wondered if she had slipped off to sleep. Susan returned at that precise moment and sighed.

"Ham and cheese melt with fries and a chocolate shake," Elaine said without even opening her eyes.

"Make that two," I said as I handed over the menus.

Susan didn't say a single word. She simply took the menus and headed away.

"That bitch ain't gonna' remember me when I'm gone," Elaine said. "But I *will* be remembered. You'll never pass a Denny's without thinking of me."

Twenty minutes later our sandwiches and shakes were gone. We were both still picking at our fries.

"You know what really sucks about dying?" Elaine asked.

I had no idea what she might say so I simply shrugged and waited.

"What sucks is knowing that I might be taking a little piece of someone else with me. I've never wanted to make anyone sad."

"Selfless to the end," I said.

"I've watched Jenna's death take something from you," she said.

There was no denying that fact.

"No matter what I tell you, you'll be a little sad. I don't want that."

"Okay, a challenge then," I said. "You have a hundred days left. By the time you go I'm going to prove to you that none of us will have even a second of sadness over it."

Elaine laughed. Susan returned with the check and asked us why we were laughing.

"Challenge accepted," Elaine said.

It was the last time that we ever shared a ham and cheese melt at Denny's.

CHAPTER 2

"All, everything that I understand,
I only understand because I love."
Leo Tolstoy

Often it was a pain in the ass. Elaine would ask to ride along as I'd drop off Tyler at school. We'd wait for her to settle into the front seat with Max squeezed in beside Tyler in the back. Elaine would speak to Tyler, asking him about his day, trying to impart some wisdom. Yeah. It was a pain in the ass; right up until the day when Elaine did not ask to come along anymore. She couldn't get out of bed, on most mornings, so life went on without her, as she had promised that it would.

On one such morning Tyler looked troubled. Max was panting in the front seat beside me and Tyler squeezed up so that his face was just inches from my right elbow as I drove.

"What happened to the guy who murdered mom?" He asked.

I thought about Albert David Fordham for the first time since yesterday.

"He's rotting in a cell," I said. "I think he's in Pennsylvania, actually."

Tyler leaned back.

"Hardly seems fair, right? He gets to eat and sleep and read and even go outside and breathe in the air, right?"

"I suppose that he does," I said.

It was a mind-numbing situation for sure, but I didn't want Tyler to lose even a moment's sleep thinking about Fordham.

"Hopefully he's suffering," Tyler said.

"He probably is," I said. "There's no greater pain than realizing that your own soul isn't worth a shit."

Tyler laughed.

"What?" I asked.

"That sounds just like grandma," he said. "I think she's wearing off on you."

We arrived at the school. Jenna's boy, who was now my son with Valerie, gathered his backpack and his lunch.

"You know what else grandma would tell you?" I asked.

Tyler waited.

"She'd tell you that you don't make the losses of yesterday be the enemy of today's win."

Tyler hoisted the pack onto his back. He offered a beautiful smile.

"I'm too tired to even think about that one," he said. "But I hope that bastard is suffering."

I sat in the car outside the school for a long time after Tyler disappeared inside. Max was panting in the seat next to me. The sun was shining bright. The fear in my heart was something that I could almost hold. The losses of yesterday were certainly threatening my wins of today and the hundreds of days ahead of me. You don't every truly get rid of the pain if you spend the rest of your days running from it. I needed to check in on Albert David Fordham, but first I had a hundred days of living to do with Elaine.

***

Elaine picked the restaurant after we explained that we weren't going to celebrate Valerie's birthday dinner at Denny's.

"Gino's Ristorante," she said, finally. "I'm looking for a piece of lasagna as big as your head."

"Gino's it is!" I said.

We were all headed for the car. Our beautiful little family was simply going out to share a meal, but with the fuse burning down on the time that we had left, we were actually savoring every minute. That is how life actually works. Minute-by-minute we make memories that allow us to strive for more. The ticking of the clock on a routine, loving day, feeds our brains as time moves forward.

"Stop!" Elaine said.

We were mere feet from the car. Elaine's one-word instruction halted us where we stood.

"Let's look around for a minute," she said.

It was a beautiful September late afternoon. The sun had shined brightly all day long, and it appeared that the evening sunset would be a glorious display of bright orange. When I gazed up at the sky I only saw a couple of small, wispy-looking clouds.

"What are we looking for?" Tyler asked. He had his hand on the door handle. "I'm hungry."

"What do you see?" Elaine asked.

"Birds, the sky, trees," Tyler said. "Can we go?"

I was starting to feel exactly what Elaine was feeling.

"I can smell the grass. I feel the ache in my legs as I think about the ground under my feet," she softly said. "I see the birds flying, but I hear them too."

Tyler was silent. I watched him close his eyes and join the little party of the senses that we were invited to by a wise old woman.

"I feel the sun on my skin," Elaine said. "It's a part of me right now. It's so beautiful."

I opened my eyes to all of what she was feeling. I chanced a look at Valerie who was holding the baby in her arms. I knew that Valerie would be crying silently, and she was. We held onto the moment for just a moment longer, and then Elaine coughed loudly to end the feeling of peace.

"That's all," she said. "Let's go get some lasagna."

***

Much later that evening we were seated around the table on the back porch. Max and Tyler were playing fetch, and while Max's heart was certainly in it, the devastation of time on his legs, made his trips back with the tennis ball, slow and almost comical. I was sipping a beer while Elaine and Valerie worked on a kettle of green tea that smelled a whole lot better than my beer.

"I had a great childhood," she said. "Life wasn't like this, for sure, but no matter how advanced we get, it's pretty much the same."

I was certainly curious to hear the explanation, but I knew enough not to press the issue with dumb questions.

"As children we spend our time running, playing, laughing. We all start out believing that the world won't crush us someday."

We had all been crushed.

Tyler was on the ground, hugging the constantly panting Max to his chest. His childhood innocence had been stolen from him way too early.

"He's gonna' be all right," I whispered.

"I know he will," Elaine said, "because he has love now. The worst kind of life to live is the one where nothing is gained or lost, right? My least favorite people are the ones who completely die while they're still alive."

I refilled Valerie and Elaine's tea, and although I knew it was a risky move, I adjusted the blanket around Elaine's feet.

"Get the hell away from me," she said with a smile in her voice.

Tyler came charging to the table with Max by his side.

"Can I take Max for a walk?" he asked.

"He's probably pooped," Valerie said. "Maybe you should let him lie down for a minute."

Yet Max seemed up for the trip around the block.

"I'll go along with you," Valerie said.

Moments later, Tyler held the leash, I held the baby, and Valerie and Tyler started their way around the block. Elaine didn't speak for a long time after they left our sight, but when she did, I could tell that she was frightened of what was to come.

"Everything you know, and everything I know, and every passing car that Max has barked at in his life is all intertwined. I've know the devil and I've known Jesus, and it's all alive in me."

Once more, I looked around and felt everything that I could possibly feel in that simple backyard. The sunset had been beautiful. The lasagna had been heavenly. We had less than a hundred days left together. We both knew that to be true, but for that moment, we were really fine with it.

"I hate that I'm afraid to close my eyes," Elaine said. "I can't stand the feeling that they may not open again in the morning, but if I go like that, just know that I've loved every minute of being alive."

I heard Max bark in the distance. I listened to the feint sound of Tyler and Valerie's laughter.

"I really love you, you know," I said and my cracking voice betrayed me a little.

"Yeah, yeah, I know," Elaine said. "Let's get inside before you cry all over yourself."

The next morning, I was the first one to open my eyes. I had a feeling that something was wrong, and a wave of panic overtook me. I was sure that Max or Elaine, or both had not made it through the night. I didn't even get dressed before I went to Tyler's room, where Max lifted his big head to acknowledge me. I hustled to Elaine's room and slowly opened the door. I didn't want to disturb her, but I had to know that she was okay.

"Not today," Elaine said from beneath the covers. "I'm still here."

"That's good," I said. "That's real good."

CHAPTER 3

*"The purpose of life is to contribute in some
way to making things better."*
Robert Kennedy

I'm not sure if I was the only one aware of it, but when I opened
my eyes on a beautiful fall morning my mind registered the thought
that it was day one-hundred-one since Elaine proclaimed that she
was in her final hundred days. Life was still moving forward, and
while her breathing was labored now and again, we were all simply
enjoying the minutes that made up our days together. We were all
well aware that she was on 'borrowed time' as Elaine liked to say,
but in the end, we are all searching for just a little more of it.

I shuffled out of the bed, wondering where Valerie was, and
leading a limping and struggling Max to the back door. My heart
wasn't quite ready for the scene that was playing out in the living
room.

Elaine was seated in the center of the couch. Valerie was at Elaine's
right side, with a laughing Juli on her lap. Tyler was on Elaine's
left. They were smashed together, laughing at the movie **Toy Story**
which was playing loudly on the large flat-screen in front of them.

"It's about time," Valerie said. "We were going to check to see if you were still breathing."

"It is day 101 after all," Elaine said.

So I wasn't the only one who'd thought about it.

I opened the sliding glass door so that Max could escape into the back yard and the cold air rushed at me. The seasons were changing once more. I watched my family seated on the couch, huddled together, laughing. Suddenly I knew exactly what I wanted to do with my day. I left Max alone to do his business and I headed to the couch and squeezed in beside Tyler. Jenna's boy wrapped an arm around my shoulder.

"This movie is funny," he said.

We sat together like that until the doorbell rang.

***

"I'm doing a story on the anniversary of the mass shooting," the pretty blonde reporter said as I opened the front door. She was trying to jumble her words together quickly so that I didn't just close her out. I had refused all requests for interviews since speaking about it with Katie Couric, but for some reason, today I left the door open.

"I'm Erica Gutterson with CNN," she said. "Please don't shut me out."

Erica batted her eyelashes and smiled, and I couldn't help but think that her beauty opened a lot of doors for her. I wasn't sure that I wanted to revisit the shooting, but maybe it was the **Toy Story** scene playing on a loop in my mind that made me do it. I invited her inside our home and I pointed at the scene in the living room.

"This is what we've been doing," I said. "We've been appreciating the gift of life."

Now I'm quite sure that Erica was trying to figure out how she could turn such a scene into a story about what had happened that tragic day, but to her credit, she did not immediately think about her ratings. Instead, for a brief moment she saw my life through my eyes.

"That's beautiful," she whispered. "That's the story we need to do."

***

We had agreed to the interview. Despite the fact that I had wanted all of us to appear on live television the next day Valerie quickly nixed that idea.

"I don't want our children on television. I don't want to be there either, but I think you need to do this."

We were seated around the kitchen table. There was a bucket of KFC in the center of the table and I was forking out a heap of mashed potatoes for Elaine's plate.

"I'm with my daughter on this one," Elaine said. "But you should be able to show people a little about living right. I've taught you enough."

"How do we do this?" I asked.

I took two chicken legs and placed them beside the potatoes and gravy.

"Two biscuits," Elaine said.

I finished up her plate and slid it across the table to her.

"How do we do this?" she repeated. "How do we make sense of the garbage that life handed us? How did we spin it into gold?"

Elaine took a healthy bite of the chicken, took a small sip of iced tea and then smiled.

"It's all about the love, stupid."

Tyler thought that was hysterical and he repeated the line about six times, but I could tell by the gleam in Elaine's eyes, as she polished off all the food I'd put on her plate, that she had a few ideas about everything I needed to say.

After dinner, Elaine sat beside me at the kitchen table. I had a notebook open and she was simply talking. I imagined that it was the sort of the way that Lennon and McCartney wrote their songs, but soon enough we had the parameters of what I needed to discuss on live television.

"We're calling this the gift of life, right," Elaine said.

"Well I'm not sure that she's gonna' ask me for a title, but that's the theme."

Elaine frowned. Today was one of her good days as she was breathing and speaking with ease. She also seemed to have more energy and she hadn't touched the oxygen much all day.

"Think about what happens to people when they suffer tragedy in their lives," she said. "The fear and the sadness blackens their heart for their remaining days. You can't do much with a black heart."

I scribbled down the words 'black heart.'

"It ain't easy living with a busted heart, is it?"

I thought of Jenna and the days we had shared. Jenna had been wild and unpredictable, but above all else, she had lived.

"A lot of people find things to take the pain away," she said. "And those things kill them. I'm thinking booze, and hatred, and bitterness."

Underneath 'black heart' I wrote 'busted heart' and the words 'what we do to survive.'

Elaine's eyes filled with tears.

"We didn't go that route," she said.

I thought about reaching out to take her hand, but I didn't. Elaine didn't respond well to sympathy.

"*Something* makes us love," she said. "Whether it's God or what's in our soul or just the way the wind blows, we, as humans, seek love and most of us rely on faith. When you reach the end, it's all that's there."

I did it anyway. I reached across the table and I placed my right hand on Elaine's left hand, which was wrinkled by time, and darkened by spots. Elaine did not recoil.

"It's about the love, stupid. Write that down, please."

I wrote: 'God', 'Soul', 'Love', and 'Faith.'

"And it's not an organized religious thing," she whispered. "I hate that shit. It's about the things we're made of that makes us want to be good."

Elaine turned her hand over and touched my hand, slowly as though she were investigating it.

"You're a good man, Sal," she said. "I want you to go out there and give the world a message from me, and then I want you to finally marry my daughter."

"I promise to do both things," I said.

"All right then. Now get your hand away from me."

Elaine and I worked on our message for another two hours, and then, for the first time ever, she allowed me to lift her into the bed.

"I'm not too fucking proud to ask for help," she said. "I just never fucking needed it until tonight."

It was a classic final sentence.

I kissed Elaine on the cheek, and left the room, tucking the notebook under my arm.

"I love you," I said.

Elaine didn't answer.

***

The next morning the camera lights flashed in my eyes. I delivered Elaine's message in the context of the mass shooting that had rocked the country nearly two years ago. Erica Gutterson did not interrupt me with questions. She simply let me talk, and I told the world everything Elaine knew about living.

"Life isn't easy. In fact, it'll beat the hell out of you if you don't stand your ground, find the love that God wills, and then somehow punch back at it. But punching back isn't quite as violent as it sounds. There are peaceful and loving ways to take a stand, and even if it seems as if you're spinning your wheels most days, you have to remain true to what is in your heart, and what bubbles below the surface.

Life is a gift. It's meant to be enjoyed so you need to laugh a little at the problems of the day. We live our lives with ourselves at the center, but we don't have to solve it like it's a crossword puzzle. We can smile our way through too. Smile every hour. It sounds simple, doesn't it? Most people don't do it.

Life is meant to be shared. Even though it really doesn't matter what other people think of you, their presence in your life is important to you, if you do it right. Can you do one nice thing for one person for one hundred days in a row? Can you offer a kind word, a reassuring thought, or that smile we talked about? Can you do that once a day for a hundred days straight? We teach kids that sharing is good, and then we forget the lesson.

Life will result in pain. The price we pay for love is pain. In our limited understanding of how everything works, we can let the pain drag us down and turn our heart black. A lot of people live their days with a black or busted heart and how they react to the pain clouds the love that they still feel. People run around chasing the pain with the love they need, and the battle never ends. Don't let the mistakes of yesterday ruin the pleasures of tomorrow. It's easy to say forgive, forget, and get over it. It's much harder to accept the pain that life provides and simply rise above it, but it needs to be done. Pain can go away in time, but only if you fill the empty space with the power that makes the sun shine, the wind blow and the leaves rustle. Pain will fester if you let it, and it will grow, and it will take over. You can't let it.

Life is meant to be lived. So live it. Smile. Forgive. Share. Do your best."

Erica had agreed to let me spread Elaine's message in an opening monologue of sorts, and as I said the words in the studio I was aware that there was a hush coming over the room. I read the words with the conviction of the love that was deep in Elaine's heart. It meant the world for me to do that. By the time that I finished Erica was trapped in a stunned silence. I imagine that she had expected me to rehash the shooting or to get into a discussion about whether or not I had forgiven Albert David Fordham. I had no desire to talk about any of that, and I didn't even have an opportunity to see if it would go that way.

As we settled into the soft red chairs in the center of the stage a man began to frantically wave to us. Another man spoke into the bug in Erica's right ear and she nodded solemnly. The cameras were off as the program headed into a unscheduled commercial break.

"You have an emergency call from your home," Erica said.

I didn't wait to get the message. Instead I retrieved my cell phone from its resting place behind stage. There were six messages from Valerie. I didn't bother listening to the messages. I knew what they were going to tell me. I hit the icon to bring Valerie's voice to my ear.

"It's Mom. She isn't breathing," she said and I heard the devastating emotion behind the mostly even voice.

"I'll be right there," I said.

"I'm in the back of the ambulance," Valerie said. "We're on our way to Sinai."

Erica was looking at me from the big red chair in the center of the stage. There was a single question racing through my mind, but I just couldn't bring myself to ask it. Valerie, as she usually does, anticipated what was in my mind.

"I don't think she'll be with us by the time you make it down there so please drive in control. The last thing she said was 'I've lived enough. I'm really tired.' "

"I love you," I tried as Elaine's final words bit into me one at a time. I knew that they would certainly try to save her life, but something deep inside told me that it was over.

Valerie had already silenced the phone.

I turned back towards the stage. Erica waved me off.

As I ran through the parking lot looking for my car, I wondered why I couldn't have just one more hour.

CHAPTER 4

"To the question of your life, you are the answer,
and to the problems of your life, you are the solution."
Joe Cordare

I was too late. Deep down, I knew that I would be. Valerie had sent me a couple of really simple texts as I made my way to Sinai Hospital.

Don't rush.

Mom loves you.

Nonetheless I rushed through the front doors and stepped into a crowded lobby. I noticed the nervous looks on the faces of the other people moving through the halls, but I was well aware that my emergency seemed somehow bigger than theirs. I spotted Valerie at a vending machine just off the main lobby. I buzzed past the information desk and arrived at her side. She was staring at the menu on the coffee machine as though it was far beyond her comprehension. She glanced up for a split-second and her eyes found me. All at once, she burst into tears and I grabbed her and pulled her to me before she could say even a single word. We just stood there, rocking back and forth, knowing that the void would never be truly filled.

"She was always my best friend," Valerie said.

"Mine too!" I answered with a laugh and a sob all rolled into one.

"She'd be pissed if she saw us blubbering," Valerie said.

"She'd tell us to 'knock it the fuck off,'" I answered.

We both laughed.

I turned my attention to the coffee machine and went through the motions of grabbing a cup for both of us as Valerie explained how easily Elaine slipped away.

"She watched you on television. She said that she was proud of you and that you nailed it. She said 'I love that man.' And then she went quiet. Tyler asked her something and she didn't answer. I knew right then that she was gone, but I just didn't want the kids to know that they'd just watched her die. I told Tyler to take Juli outside for a minute and I called 911. Once we got here it was just a matter of procedure. She died at home. They asked me to give them a half an hour or so. We can say good-bye together."

I led Valerie to two hard plastic chairs in a mostly empty waiting room. I thought about Tyler and all the death he'd seen in his short time on the planet. He was supposed to be a child. He wasn't supposed to be caught up in such despair.

"How is Tyler going to deal with another death?" I asked.

"As we do," Valerie said. "Mom spent the last few months of her life talking to Tyler as much as she talked to you."

"Of course she did," I said.

"You should have heard her. She said some beautiful things," Valerie said.

"I did hear her," I said. "She was a hell-of-a woman."

***

The funeral was over. The gathering finished the final prayer from behind us. The crisp cold air was a bad mix with the tears, the running nose and the pain that was pulsating in the center of my chest. Valerie's left hand was trapped in my right, and she held fast to Juli while Tyler crowded my left side. The boy was nearly sitting in the same seat as me in front of Elaine's beige casket. Twenty minutes from now that casket would be lowered to its final resting spot some six feet below the ground we were standing on. All at once, a loud, guttural sob escaped Tyler's little body.

I turned quickly.

The anguished look on his face told me that he was no longer able to hold any of it in.

"Where do they go?" he whispered through his tears.

I turned to Valerie. She knew just what I was asking and simply nodded. I took Tyler's hand and led him away from the cemetery scene.

"We can stay here," Tyler said.

"Nah, let's take a little walk," I whispered.

Elaine would've been proud to see the amount of people who gathered to attend her funeral. We brushed by a number of them and headed down a clear path that led us to a wooded area.

"I'm sorry," Tyler said. "I'm just gonna' really miss her, you know?"

"I do know," I said. "I'm gonna' miss her too."

In the relative quiet of our walk through the trees the world seemed a lot bigger to me all of a sudden. Birds were floating through the air, leaves were rustling in the soft wind, and the sun was trying to edge its way clear of the heavy clouds.

"Will she watch me? Do Mom and Dad watch me?"

I wasn't quite sure how to answer such questions. The mysteries of life should remain mysteries to children.

"I don't know," I said. "It's impossible to know everything, right?"

"Grandma said that she'd always be with me somehow. She said I could carry her with me in my heart."

Tyler's tears rolled down his soft cheeks. The one thing that I wanted for him was for him to grieve deeply. Yet Elaine had left him with a thought so beautiful that I could not add much to it.

"That's really true," I said. "We can carry the people we love with us no matter where we go. I'll talk to Grandma every day. I'll feel her in my heart and in my mind. I'll always know what she might say."

Tyler laughed through his tears.

"She'll probably swear!"

We stopped walking and just stood in the center of the dirt path. I tousled Tyler's blonde hair and he smiled up at me.

"I don't want you or Valerie or Max or Juli to go," he whispered.

"I'm not going anywhere for a long time," I said, but as the words left my mouth I knew that I had no way of guaranteeing such a thing. Tyler had already suffered so much in such a short period of time.

"We have to keep going, right?" I asked, lamely.

"It's going to take a lot of love," Tyler said.

Those eight words did it. I knelt in front of Jenna's son, and I pulled him to me. He was my son. He was Valerie's little boy, and he was absolutely right. It was going to take a lot of love, and right then, right there, with the cars pulling away from the cemetery, in the distance, I felt Elaine deep in my heart.

"We have a ton of love to carry with us," I whispered.

I felt Tyler's tears on my cheek.

"I love you, Dad," he said.

***

Later that night we held one another in bed. Valerie had never looked more drained, but she was all cried out. She rested her head on my chest and we silently lay there, just staring up at the ceiling.

"She left a note for you," Valerie said. "I didn't know if you'd want to read it today, or wait. She told me to wait to give it to you. 'Until she was worm food,' she said."

"I'd like to read it in the morning," I said. "Tonight I just want to hold you."

Valerie sighed heavily. She cuddled even closer and offered a faint smile. The bullet had stripped her of her full smile and while she was conscious of the subtle change to her face, it did not seem to concern her. She was here with me. We had rebuilt our family.

"Will you marry me?" I whispered.

"It's about time you asked," she whispered back.

And then we fell to sleep like that. We were certainly heartbroken, but we knew what it would take to move forward.

It was going to take a lot of love.

***

The next morning, Max circled a tree in the back yard. The sun was making its ascent and even though it was a bit chilly with a slight breeze sweeping across the porch, I sipped a coffee in a brown lawn chair. The letter was unopened before me. Three letters were scripted on the plain white envelope: 'S-A-L'.

I pictured Elaine in her chair with the pad and pen. I considered how sick she was and how she knew that her time left would be counted in hours rather than weeks or months or years. What a strange feeling that must be. Some people don't get the chance to put their affairs in order. Elaine was straightening all of us up long before the terrorist attack in front of Outback.

Max's limping stilted effort to get back to my chair brought a wave of sadness to my heart. Every living thing will eventually break down. Max plopped his huge head into my lap and I rubbed his ears.

"Who's a good boy?"

Max leaned into my touch as Tyler's words once again made a beeline to my brain. Everything I knew about getting through this was based in love and if we needed a lot of love to battle it, we'd throw even more than that at it.

"I love you, buddy," I said to Max.

I brushed the tears away and picked up the envelope. I traced my fingers across those three letters printed on the front and edged my index finger to loosen the flap. Knowing Elaine, I didn't believe the letter would be lengthy and it wasn't. There were five simple sentences there.

You know how I've loved you. I'm asking you to move forward by writing a book about Fordham with forgiveness, and peace in your heart. Marry my daughter, you idiot, and love those children! I have bigger and better things to attend to now. You know everything there is to know about living.

I read the letter again, and again, and again. I laughed at her mention of the fact that I was an idiot and I yearned to tell her that I'd asked Valerie to marry me just last night. I cried when I read that she was off to attend to bigger and better things. Elaine was great at making me laugh and cry all at once.

Max's leisurely stay by the side of my chair ended abruptly as a squirrel invaded our space by walking along the top of the green fence and plopping down in the back corner of the yard. The limp was suddenly gone as Max headed straight for the scrambling squirrel. There was no chance that Max would get there in time, but the effort was still there. The life is in the chase.

CHAPTER 5

"We are all shaped and fashioned by those we love."
Geothe

Two days later I was in the car, stuck in traffic, talking to my editor on the blue tooth. His voice was coming to me loud and clear. He was begging me to do something I had already decided to do. I had always enjoyed working with John Paige. Despite the fact that he hadn't been my most ardent of supporters he had always worked hard for his pay check, and now he was trying to keep the whole concept of a daily newspaper afloat, or so he thought.

"We need you to give *us* the story on Fordham," he said for the third time.

"I'm going to do a book," I explained. "I promised Elaine that I'd bring it to some sort of conclusion."

"I'd rather you did a series of feature stories, but okay, we'll do the buildup, we'll print excerpts. You gotta' throw me a bone here."

I didn't figure that I had to throw him anything, but I had every intention of helping the paper in any way I could. Elaine and Valerie had taught me the lessons of loyalty. Paige spent the next ten minutes filling me in on Fordham's prison life.

The Lewisburg penitentiary is a high-security prison with a general population of about 1,400 inmates. It had once been home to Whitey Bulger, John Gotti, Jimmy Hoffa and even American authors Samuel Roth and Ralph Ginzburg, who had been imprisoned for obscenity. Paige was filling me in on the dynamics of the prison, but I had spent the evening before watching the 1991 Academy-Award documentary, *Doing time: Life inside the Big House* by filmmakers Alan and Susan Raymond.

It looked as if Fordham was suffering enough.

Fordham was stationed in the Special Management Unit of the prison. He had been deemed as one of the most violent and disruptive guests.

I thought of all of this after disconnecting with Paige. We'd cover more ground when I got to his office. What would have happened to us had Fordham not interfered? Life had changed for all of us. Since Elaine's death we had continued to wrap ourselves in love and family and togetherness. Was I opening a can of worms? Did I really need to pry into the mind of Fordham to solve the riddles in my own mind? What the hell did I know about anything, anyway?

I was about to find out.

***

Paige was up and out of his chair quickly.

"I've never seen you move that fast," I said as I extended my hand.

Paige's beard was scruffy. There were red rims around his eyes and he patted his stomach as he moved back to his chair.

"Before you even say it, I'm still a mess," he said. "I drink too much, eat bad shit, and work long hours to try and save this sinking ship. Why don't people read the newspaper anymore? You see them all looking down at their tiny phones. We're gonna' have a lot of blind people someday. I don't know how they do it. Wouldn't you rather feel the paper in your hands? I do."

"Are you done?" I asked. "I'm about to write a book. I feel your pain. Who do you know that still reads books?"

Paige looked to the ceiling.

"It'll come back around," he said. "People will see the error of their ways."

We both chuckled.

"Are you okay?" Paige asked. "How the hell did you survive everything?"

"Sink or swim," I said. "A minute at a time."

"Horrible, just horrible," Paige said. "I know how deeply you felt for Jenna…and Elaine."

I didn't actually have an answer.

"Tell me about Fordham," I said.

Paige got started. He spoke for a solid twenty minutes, filling me in on the psychiatric testing, the guilty plea and the reason why they weren't going to put him to death.

"He bought himself a permanent home at the Big House," he said. "If you can break down why a life heads in that direction I'd appreciate if you'd share it with the world."

"There's no good reason, I suppose," I said. "But I'm heading up there to see. I owe it to everyone he obliterated. The suffering he created is monumental."

"I'll go with you," Paige said as we stood at the door, shaking hands good-bye.

"No, thanks," I said, "And not because I don't want the stench of double cheeseburgers in my car."

We both smiled.

"I have to do this alone."

"I understand," Paige said. "Make sure that fucker knows how hated he is."

***

Yet as I drove I thought about Paige's words and I knew that such an approach might feed Fordham exactly what he needed. Fordham would get off on knowing the destruction he caused. He had set out to destroy. Eventually I needed to show him that collectively we were still standing.

I hardly noticed the two-and-a-half-hour drive to the prison in Lewisburg, Pennsylvania. Instead my mind worked through a movie of Jenna's life. I considered the moment when we first met, first kissed, first held one another. The sound of her laughter echoed through the recesses of my mind. I considered how broken she felt when we realized that our child had died. Every single possible aspect of Jenna's being alive was present in my heart and mind. I felt pure beauty as I exited the highway on my way to visiting absolute hatred. I was also carrying Valerie, Tyler, Juli and Elaine with me. The car was full.

If I hadn't known better, I would've thought that I was entering a college campus instead of one of the most talked about state lockups. The beautifully landscaped grounds, and the recently reworked buildings looked shiny and new. From the outside it didn't look as if Fordham was in such a bad place, but I knew that the secrets were trapped inside the walls.

I headed to the information desk. A security guard eyed me as I moved ahead down the long white corridor.

"I'm Sal Pisceo," I said to the tiny Asian woman behind the huge desk. I slid my driver's license and press pass across the desk and she smiled.

"You're all set," she said. "They just called down wondering if you'd arrived. The prisoner is already in the waiting area."

Paige had done all the hard work. I simply had to walk in, sit down, and understand.

***

Albert David Fordham was dressed in an orange jumpsuit. His legs, hands and mid-section were shackled. He was seated at a table, smoking a cigarette, and sipping a coffee. He looked fairly content. His eyes followed me from my first step in the door to my chair directly across from him at the table.

"Are you suffering enough?" Fordham asked.

His voice was gravelly and the laughter that he forced sent him into a coughing jag. He took another hit from the cigarette.

"I'm not suffering much," I said. I waved my hands in front of me. "See, full range of motion."

Fordham's countenance was one of mild annoyance.

"How about you?" I asked. "Is it absolutely horrendous in here? I hope so."

I was feeding the beast a bit, but I had no intention of ever becoming friends with Fordham. Elaine's memory was pressing forgiveness, but I didn't have to not hate the asshole.

"You find the torture that you're comfortable with," Fordham said. "These bastards think they're cute by tightening the cuffs so that it's cutting off circulation, but what can you do? I live with it. I don't let 'em see me sweat. Same thing with the skinheads, the Aryans, the brothers. They can try and get to me, but *no one* gets to me."

Fordham had earned a few favors by agreeing to cooperate with me, but I don't believe that it would've taken much coaxing. He was ready to talk.

"Have they given you the tour?" Fordham asked.

"Not yet," I said. "I'm here to gather your wisdom."

"Well they won't show you the dark areas anyway. I'm in SMU. They don't take visitors up that way. They don't want you to see the fucking rats, spiders, or cramped halls. They won't show you the walls where the lead paint is flaking off, poisoning us. They won't show you the fucking gourmet meals they expect us to eat."

Fordham was working himself up into a regular lather. I knew that he was pushing his own agenda, thinking that perhaps my writing could shine a light on how poorly we were treating our criminals. I wasn't much interested in that angle.

"Am I supposed to feel bad for you?" I asked.

Fordham didn't respond. He ground his cigarette out on the table and placed it in the ashtray. Each movement came with the sound of the clanging chains and his irritated expression.

"We're all in a cage," he said. "Mine is just a physical one. You were the guy who was banging that actress, right? It must've been tough to know that I shot her right through the fucking head. She was a pretty girl. I'm sorry about that. It was nothing personal."

The need to detach from his words was necessary, but the wry smile on his face was absolutely infuriating, of course. I swallowed hard and Fordham caught it and his smile brightened.

"You'll have to answer to God," I said.

"God! God! Are you fucking kidding me? God!" Fordham's deep laughter echoed off the walls. He moved his hand up to pretend to wipe tears from his eyes.

"That's a hot one," he said. "God! Fuck! Is this going to be one of those 'Forgive the bad guy because God wants us to' books?"

I was sure not to respond to Fordham's little outburst. Instead, I studied him. He had a soul patch, was tattooed up and down his arms and on the left side of his neck. It appeared that he had covered himself in snakes. There was also a tear drop under his right eye. He had deep, penetrating brown eyes that showed absolute rage. He was just about what I had expected.

"There's nothing original about you," I said. "You're the perfect piece of shit that I expected."

Fordham took the shot well.

"This is how **God** made me," he said.

He reached for another cigarette. I followed his hands and he looked to the door. One of the conditions of his speaking with me was that he would be allowed to smoke as many cigarettes as he wanted. I didn't care. I waited for the guard to enter the room and light the Marlboro for him. He took a long drag and the smoke billowed around his eye.

"What do you want from me, *Sally*," he asked. "Do you wanna' know about my mommy and daddy? I didn't have either. Do you wanna' know if I hate America, or the African-American in the White House?"

He laughed uproariously.

"Eventually," I said. "Something *had* to drive the hate."

Fordham considered it for a moment.

"Actually I did it only because I *felt* like it," he said. "I never met a person that meant a single fucking thing to me. I've never felt anything else but hate. So, fuck you. I did it because I *felt* like it."

It struck me suddenly that there wasn't much inside of the man across the table. He was a shell of a human being. The soul that we are all blessed to have was vacant inside of him. There was no way that I could forgive him.

"You don't have many questions," Fordham said. "You don't even have a notebook."

I continued to stare at him. I was taking photos in my mind. Elaine's voice was torturing me to *understand* how to forgive him.

"You didn't kill those people just to see what it felt like," I finally said. "That's pure bullshit."

Fordham didn't answer. I wasn't going to wait around for it anyway. I pressed the buzzer that they had provided and the guards entered quickly.

"That's it?" Fordham asked.

"I'll be back," I said. "Get some answers straight. We're all done with the tough guy stare down."

I headed out into the hallway. I wanted to get back to my family.

"Two fucking cigarettes," Fordham said. "That's garbage!"

They led him down the hallway. The sound of his chains clanging vibrated off the walls.

"Be ready to talk next time, *Sally*," he called out.

That's what hate looks like, I thought.

I couldn't get out of there fast enough. How does one fill themselves with hatred? I knew that if I found that answer I would be able to begin the search to forgive. Elaine's lessons were ricocheting through my brain. I busted through the front door of the prison and gazed up at the cloudy sky and the low ceiling pressing down on me.

"I'm trying," I yelled. "I'm really trying."

CHAPTER 6

"With love one can live even without happiness."
Fydor Dostoyevsky

Tyler's throwing motion was not yet fully developed. He'd often follow through in an exaggerated manner which, when I was a kid, led someone to scream out about 'throwing like a girl.' Evidently life hadn't changed much in the world of pre-adolescent boys because Tyler had been taking some heat from his 'friends'. He didn't want to throw like a girl.

I was down in a crouch, coaching Tyler to throw the ball, directly at the glove. He was doing his best imitation of the Orioles closer Zach Britton, and tossing the ball as hard as he could. Pitch after pitch, encouraging word after encouraging word, and Tyler's motion was becoming more compact. He was starting to throw the ball in a fluid manner, and there was actually some speed on the ball.

"You're doing great," I said as I brought myself up to a standing position. My knees were creaking loudly and my first two steps away were painful.

"I love baseball," he said.

I had to do it. I lifted his cap and tousled his hair. It was such a

Dad thing to do and I understood why the first Dad did it. There was a true connection and showing affection for those you love is the first step in making them believe that they are secure in the world.

Albert David Fordham was never far from my mind during the waking moments of my day, and there had been nights when he had even invaded my sleep. The first trip to the prison had allowed me to see him, hear his voice, and feel the disdain. The next visit would allow me to dig deeper. I would get the information that I needed to forgive him because Tyler needed me, and I wasn't going to raise him with even a trace of hatred in my heart.

"Are we still going out tonight?" Tyler asked as we headed through the back door and into the house. Max lifted his head but didn't get up. Tyler went straight to him.

"Yeah, Mom needs a break. We're going to buy her a nice dinner, anywhere she wants to go."

"I asked her," Tyler said. "She said we're going to Denny's so she can get a ham and cheese melt."

I laughed.

"That's perfect!"

I spent the next twenty minutes getting ready. As I showered and dressed I completely forgot about playing catch. I thought only of Fordham and his childhood. I also thought about Valerie, and love.

***

Fordham, despite his claim, did indeed have a mother and father. They were colossal pieces of shit, mind you, but they certainly did exist. Fordham's childhood home was a mobile trailer unit in a broken down section of Dundalk. Fordham's mother, who went by the name Ginger Fordham, was a teenage girl who quit school at sixteen and spent some time at a local strip club, where she worked with her own mother. The family business, I suppose. Fordham's father, Juan Gonzales, was a patron of the strip joint who earned his money the old-fashioned way, by dealing drugs, to his new girlfriend's former school mates. There was no love between Juan, a six-feet-four-inch bodybuilder, and Ginger, a fiery redhead with a love for methamphetamine.

It was about what I'd expected.

Social services began snooping around the living arrangement when Albert was just a baby. Ginger had once left the child in a car as she gambled at a race track. Inexplicably she was granted probation for the offense. Albert was returned to the home, but not for long. He quit school at the age of fourteen and left the trailer on the same day. Neither Ginger or Juan bothered to look for him. Social services had lost track. The school stopped calling. Albert was free to do anything he pleased.

Like his Dad, Albert grew to a pretty good size. He was an intimidating factor early on and it helped him as he built a career selling drugs to a lot of the people Juan sold them to. Albert had taken up the family business, but Juan wasn't a fan of the move. His son was moving in on his customers. So Juan tracked down his boy, and beat him half to death. Juan was never arrested for the beating and Albert failed to cooperate with the police who investigated it. Albert didn't need anyone's help. Currently, no one knows what happened to Juan. He hasn't been seen in years. As for Ginger, she still resides in Dundalk. The arrest of her boy brought her a bit of fame and she tried desperately to parlay it into some sort of career, but superstardom is elusive when you're a strung-out, dope-addled, whore. Ginger hadn't been on Albert's hit list, as far as anyone knew, but I was certain that her name would elicit a response.

"Are we ready to go?" Valerie asked.

She stood before me, dressed casually for our trip to Denny's. She was wearing a GAP sweatshirt and a pair of tan jeans. She opened her arms wide and I stepped into them.

"Thinking of Fordham?"

"A little," I said. "His childhood wasn't ideal."

"They never are. Still, millions of kids have lousy childhoods and they don't murder people."

"Granted," I said.

I kissed Valerie, lingering for a long moment, as her soft lips took me a million miles away from the trailer in Dundalk.

"Yuck!" Tyler called out. "Stop kissing!"

I made a grand gesture of kissing Valerie again. I thought of something I'd read a long while ago. *The best thing I could do for my children was show them love for their mother.*

Valerie wasn't Tyler's mother, but close enough. I doubted that Albert ever busted in on Ginger and Juan sharing a loving moment.

"It's funny, but my mouth has been watering for a ham and cheese melt all week!" Valerie said.

"I hear you," I said. "Elaine hears you too."

Max joined the fray as Tyler tried to pull me and Valerie apart. Val reached down and patted Max's head.

"The fur ball grew on you, huh?" I asked.

"Oh I've always loved Max," she said.

We both laughed.

Love is such a simple word, but it really is a hard concept to grasp. Tyler and Max headed for the front door. Valerie touched my arm to get me to halt.

"Did Fordham's parents abuse him?" she asked.

"I don't know," I said.

"That would be the only thing," she said. "That might make me eventually forgive a little."

"I'm not sure he'll talk about it if it did happen," I said. "He's a real peach."

***

The waitress was an unbelievably cute young girl who introduced herself as Nicole. Tyler immediately paid attention to Nicole's smile and he sounded an awful lot like Elaine when he spoke to her.

"You're really pretty when you smile," he said.

Nicole's face lit up.

"Wow! You're my favorite customer ever," she said.

Nicole continued to smile as she set place mats for us and helped Valerie get Juli into the child seat. She also gave me a quick wink, knowing exactly what needed to happen as the ham and cheese melts were delivered to the table. We had worked up the entire plan a full day ahead of time.

"We don't need our menus," Tyler said. "We all want ham and cheese melts with fries and a chocolate milk, right?"

"Right," Valerie said.

"Perfect," Nicole said.

Valerie was leaning across, placing crackers that she'd brought from home, in front of Juli. I shot a glance to Nicole, again, wordlessly asking if we were all set. Nicole gave me a thumbs-up sign that

Tyler didn't miss. I put a finger to my nose to keep Tyler quiet. He nodded. He knew exactly what was going on, but despite his excitement, he kept quiet. Nicole rubbed the top of his head and smiled again. She turned and headed toward the kitchen, with my engagement ring in her bright red apron.

The time between placing our order and their arrival at our table was eternal. I had no idea why I was so nervous, Valerie had certainly agreed to marry me, but placing the ring beside the ham and cheese melt was going to send her into a crying fit, and I sincerely hoped that they were tears of happiness and not sadness over missing her beautiful mother.

Nicole returned with the tray of chocolate milk and placed them carefully before all of us. Juli's milk was white and in a sippy cup. Our daughter cupped it and brought it to her mouth with a quick giggle that made all of us laugh.

"What a beautiful family," Nicole said.

If she only knew how difficult the formation of the family had been, but I didn't think of the pain as we waited. Instead I focused on how perfect it all seemed at the moment. Fordham's act of destruction had resulted in the beauty before me. It was strange how life worked.

Valerie and Tyler began to color the menu. Tyler completed the maze first although I think that Valerie let it happen that way. They were both in mid-laugh when Nicole returned with the plates of food. Nicole placed meals in front of Tyler and me. She then stopped and feigned confusion.

"Oh God! I forgot yours," she said to Valerie. "I'll be right back!"

Valerie, who had been waiting for the sandwich, looked a tad befuddled.

"Take mine," I said.

The ring was glistening beside the sandwich on my plate.

"No," Valerie said. "Go ahead, I'll wait."

I slid the plate across the table and gave it a 180-degree spin as I did so, bringing the ring to full view.

"I promise to put your needs first," I said. "If you'll promise to be my wife."

"Do it! Do it!!" Tyler said, right on cue. "You know you want to!"

Tyler had pulled it off just as we had practiced. I laughed, and Valerie cried. Nicole was back with the final ham and cheese melt as a sob escaped Valerie's body.

"Mom would be so happy," she said. "Of course I'll marry you."

I was up and out of the chair and I kissed her mouth. She'd been shot in the face, but she never looked more beautiful than she did on that moment. I hugged her for all I was worth, and then wrapped her close with Tyler and Juli fully involved in our embrace.

"I love you," I whispered.

"I love you too," Valerie answered, "But I'm imagining Mom right now. She'd be yelling 'eat the f-ing sandwiches before they get cold.'"

We ate the ham and cheese melts and drank the chocolate milk as the Denny's crew offered their congratulations.

It was a perfect meal.

CHAPTER 7

"You were put on this earth to achieve your greatest self,
to live out your purpose, and to do it fearlessly."
Steve Maraboli – Life, the Truth & Being Free.

This time the drive to the prison was filled with less trepidation. Fordham was not a man to be feared. In fact, he was just a sorry human being that was not worthy of much consideration. I made the drive with a heart filled with the excitement of marrying Valerie and in sharing my days with the family we now had. I considered Jenna and what might have happened had Fordham not entered our lives, but there was no room in my head for such a thought. I still loved Jenna, as I always would. Fordham took her from me, physically, but he could never touch the love in my heart. Still in all, as I parked my car, I felt a twinge of pure hatred for Fordham and men like them. I really needed to drive the hate away.

Once more Fordham was waiting for me in the same empty room. His chains rattled as I entered the room as he struggled to get into a more comfortable position. He was still in the red jump suit and there were still heavy bags under his eyes. His cigarette was already burning and he was blowing rings of smoke into the space above his head.

"Morning, Sally," he said. "Did you ever just not **give a fuck**?"

I sat down slowly as I contemplated his shouted question. He most certainly practiced that question over and over in his small cell so there had to be a reason why he immediately posed it to me.

"No," I said. "I've always been able to find a reason to care even on my darkest of days."

Fordham let the answer sink in. He took another long drag and blew more smoke.

"You're a better man than me," he said.

He struggled to sit up a little straighter and he brought his hands to the front of his body and leaned in.

"I been thinking," he said. "I never really learned right from wrong or how to give two shits about anyone other than me."

I thought about his childhood. Ginger and Juan hadn't actually put it all together for him, but he didn't appear to be looking for sympathy.

"I'm just saying that there are millions of people like me. We're just garbage to people like you. You kick fifty bucks to a homeless shelter at Christmas to help the poor and then you go on your way."

Fordham motioned for the guard so that he could get another cigarette lit. It occurred to me that he had spent a portion of his time contemplating why he had murdered people. Fordham was searching for the reason as much as I was, and of course, he knew the difference between right and wrong.

"You're sorry now, aren't you?" I asked.

"You're looking at it through your eyes again," Fordham said. "You have to imagine **me**. You have to imagine being so filled with anger that you can't see straight. There are minutes when I'm sorry, but then the anger returns."

I certainly believed that. Fordham was a mess from day one. I tried my best, as he sat there before me, to imagine being him. We weren't quite as different as one might think.

"We're all the same," I said. "We all search for the same things in life. We all need to be a part of something or to be loved by someone."

Fordham's face broadened as he smiled from ear-to-ear.

"I knew you'd start spewing your bullshit," he said. "I read all your whiny little columns. *Everything you know!*

I let Fordham finish making fun of me. I even watched as the cigarette he smoked was reduced to a nub. Then I leaned close to him.

"Life isn't easy for anyone," I said. "I know the deck was stacked against you. I realize that you have the mental capabilities of a small child. I know that you are angry, but you *knew* what you were doing that day."

Fordham grimaced at the start of my speech, and quickly that grimace turned into a sarcastic smile, but I kept going.

"You wanted to inflict pain because you'd been in pain every single minute of your sorry life. That's a shame. It really is, but here's the thing, Albert. Love can grow in the darkest of places, and it can fill the emptiest of hearts."

Fordham actually chuckled when I said that, but there was a minor disturbance happening behind his dark eyes.

I pushed forward.

"You laugh at the notion of God, you scoff at the idea of peace, and you mock the rest of us who strive to live right, but there is something inside you that wants to be noticed. When you emptied that gun you weren't just acting on the hate in your heart, you were also searching for love."

Fordham guffawed loudly. I waited until his laughter died out, realizing that while he was laughing at me, he wasn't answering me.

"I know what I'm saying doesn't make any sense to you, and you're right, we should be embarrassed, as a society, that we let people like you fester and grow, but make no mistake about it, you were searching for something to fill your heart. Unfortunately, you're a coward, and instead of trying to better yourself, you did a fucked up math equation where you tried to subtract the love that other people had so that you could even the score."

"Fuck you," he whispered.

"Here's the thing with love, Albert."

I paused for a full minute and he smoked and smiled, waiting for my big finish.

"You can't take it from people," I said, leaning even closer to his sorry face. "You should have tried to find some depth in your world, and if you were hell bent on subtracting, you should've simply subtracted yourself, but you were too cowardly to do that because you wanted to stick around and see if you could somehow, someway find some satisfaction in your horrid existence."

I was whispering. Fordham was taking each sentence as a punch.

"I'm going to give you some satisfaction," I said. "I forgive you."

"I don't need your forgiveness," he said.

I ignored him.

"Take what I've given you back to your cell and chew on it for the next however the fuck long you're in here. I forgive you. Elaine forgave you, Valerie will someday forgive you, and Jenna…"

I faded out at the mention of Jenna's name. She most likely would have *never* forgiven Fordham. The mere fact that the pile of garbage before me had ended her life made me sad enough to just stop speaking. Fordham sensed that my entire speech was null and void as his action had trumped what I knew in my mind to be true.

"Janna maybe not?" Fordham asked, playfully.

"Jenna would've never forgiven you," I said. "And it's not important that she wouldn't. You got what you wanted out of that as well. You spread your hate."

Fordham fell back into the chair. He rubbed the cigarette out in the ashtray as he motioned for the guard.

"Fuck you," he whispered. "Don't come back here."

"I don't need to," I said.

"GET ME THE FUCK OUT!" Fordham yelled.

Two guards entered the room and Fordham got to his feet.

"*Everything I Know,*" he said. "You're a fucking idiot."

I stood to face him. We were mere inches apart.

"That's the thing," he said. "You've spent your life just as confused as me. You chose love. I chose hate. Who knows who's right?"

Fordham was ushered out the door. His laughter was once more echoing off the walls as he shuffled down the corridor.

"Good riddance," I whispered to his back.

"Fuck you, Sally," he cried out.

Less than three weeks later Albert David Fordham was found face down in the prison yard. There was just a single stab wound, but the knife had pierced his heart. The Big House had claimed one more. Someone had taken a stand against hate. The assailant was never found. It had been Fordham's first appearance with the general population.

He died the day before my wedding.

CHAPTER 8

"We are all shaped and fashioned by those we love."
-Goethe

Valerie didn't walk down an aisle in the traditional sense. In fact, she strutted across the outfield grass, holding Juli in her right arm. Valerie was dressed in an Orioles jersey with 'Ripken' written across her back. Tyler stood beside me wearing a matching orange and black shirt with 'Britton' on the back. I was in the Orioles white jersey with red lettering and my name of choice was 'Robinson'. I didn't care much if people thought it was to honor either Frank or Brooks.

Juli was wearing an O's onesie and there was a bit of caked formula on the black bird's beak on the front of the garment. Valerie was working on removing the stain when she arrived by my side in front of the justice of the peace. There were only about fifty people standing in the outfield grass with us, as witnesses to our marriage.

"What a beautiful day," Justice Ward whispered. "What a beautiful family."

It occurred to me that we were doing things a little differently. There weren't any church bells ringing. We hadn't planned on a reception at a hall with a limo and a huge cake. It was just me and my family, and my love.

We had even written our own vows.

"Are we ready?" Justice Ward asked.

Juli laughed as Valerie tickled her neck and the Justice smiled along with everyone else.

"I take that as a 'yes'," he said.

*****

Much later that night I woke with a start. Valerie was snoring lightly on her side of the bed. In the darkness I could not see the beauty of her sleeping form, but I could feel it. In fact, I felt it in every bone in my body. I sat on the edge of the bed, recalling how she had cried when she spoke her vows of love.

"Everything is nothing and nothing is everything," she had said. "And none of life means anything at all unless we inject our love into it. Then it means **everything**. Life is like a book on a coffee table…unless you grab it and open it and see what's inside, it'll just sit there, and it won't mean anything. Our job, as a couple, as a family, is to simply enjoy the little moments, and share the happiness, the sadness and the terror that life will bring, because those little moments will all add up to something **big**, if we make it happen."

Valerie had made it all the way through the start of her vows without crying, but her eyes filled quickly when she continued.

"I spent a lot of years trapped in my own head," she told the gathering. "When life struck me, point-blank, I was forced to ask myself what was most important, and then I had the courage to build my life around the love in my heart. I vow to figure out what to do, with you as my love and then together we will do it."

I hadn't even waited for Justice Ward to tell me to kiss the bride. I kissed her right then and there and the ceremony was halted for a few moments as we cried together, in front of our children, and the gathering.

I won't have enough days to tell her how much I love her.

I stepped out of the darkness of our bedroom, on our wedding night. I patted my leg and Max came to attention. He followed me out of the bedroom and out onto the back porch. My old, tired dog sniffed around in the grass in the silence of the pre-dawn. There was a soft breeze sweeping across the lawn chairs, the wind chimes and me. I looked to the star-filled sky, thinking of Elaine, Jenna, my parents, and everyone who actually had shared a moment of my journey up to that point. I even thought of Fordham and how the evil in his heart had invaded my life.

Everything is nothing and nothing is everything unless we inject our love into it.

It was all I really needed to know.

I heard the sliding glass door open and close behind me.

I worked quickly to wipe the tears from my eyes.

"Are you okay?" Valerie whispered.

"I'm perfect," I said.

She sat in my lap.

There in the darkness, with the wind touching us lightly, we held one another and cried until we laughed.

ACKNOWLEDGEMENTS

When I first started writing I would work with my sister, Carrie Lynn, to brainstorm the story ideas. We both got busy and my brainstorming was done alone, but every single time I start a story I think about the readers who might help me as I'm going along. Thankfully, I have a few, and Carrie Lynn remains a faithful pre-reader.

I'd like to thank Cathy Weiser, Lynn Lombard and especially David Bagnall for helping me with 'Everything I Know'.

All three offered invaluable help, and David was especially helpful with a reminder that basically told me to 'slow down' a little.

I enjoyed writing this one, and will especially enjoy every single person who mentions that 'Everything I Know' will certainly be a short book.

That's the lesson.

My son, as a toddler, used to say, 'It's not your world, you know.'

Lesson learned.

Thanks to all who helped!

Made in the USA
Middletown, DE
19 December 2018